SEVEN PRINCES OF HELL

"Saul"

SEVEN PRINCES OF HELL: SAUL

Copyright © 2019 Samantha Cummings.

All rights reserved. No part of this publication may be reproduced, distributed, or transmitted in any form or by any means, including photocopying, recording, or other electronic or mechanical methods, without the prior written permission of the publisher, except in the case of brief quotations embodied in critical reviews and certain other non-commercial uses permitted by copyright law. For permission requests, write to the publisher, addressed "Attention: Permissions Coordinator," at the email address below.

Any references to historical events, real people, or real places are used fictitiously. Names, characters, and places are products of the author's imagination.

Front cover image by Samantha Cummings.

ASIN: B07Y4WWQND (e-book)

ISBN: 9781712445440

Published in Great Britain by Amazon.

First published edition 2019.

www.samantha-cummings.com

SEVEN PRINCES OF HELL

"Saul"

Frances June

Chapter 1

If the rats don't kill you the demons will. Maybe not real demons but the emotionally manipulative, ancient-history kind. The ones that call you up outta the blue at 3 a.m to tell you your baby brother's been murdered and left for dead, floating face down near pier 90 all the way down on 54th.

The cigarette hanging from my lips glows too bright for this time in the day. I hardly inhale because I'm trying to quit but sometimes the smoke just slips between my teeth and licks its way into my lungs; the burn is good, the buzz not so much. It's too early on an empty, whiskey-less stomach, but I don't put it out.

No coat is thick enough or warm enough for New York winters but I still try to pull my coat closer around me whilst I wait for the cab to arrive. Even at 5a.m the streets smell like too many people and garbage. Morgan didn't stir when I got the phone call so I left her sleeping upstairs. She'll be pissed when she sees I sent her a text to explain why my side of the bed will be cold when she checks. She never liked Billy when he was alive so she's going to be less than impressed when she finds out his corpse pulled me back into the fold.

If I'm honest, I didn't like him all too much either but family duty screams louder than Morgan when she smells smoke on my breath.

Christ, this morning is cold. It takes longer than I'd like to check the time on my phone; 5:15 and Ash is as late as he always is. When the cab idles around the corner my hands feel like ice blocks. If I wanted hands as yellow as the cab I'd consider actually holding the cigarette but it tempted me too much; the pull, the flicking, the repetition in the ritual that I keep trying so hard to kick.

Without using my hands I drop the butt and dig it into the concrete with my toe. There's something satisfying in the scrape of rubber against concrete; I picture digging my heal into someone's hand until the satisfaction of the crunching and screaming ignites a siren in the distance.

There it is, one of those demons that lingers, threateningly, always around the corner ready to kill.

"You ready?"

Ash mouths the words at me through the window, too smart to roll it down and let the frost in the air freeze his dick off. His most prized possession.

All I can do is nod and wait for him to slide over to the other side of the cab. Even though it's petty I enjoy the fact that the sweat-crusted leather might trash his $300 pants. Even from outside the cab he looks like he's dressed for a meeting in Wall Street.

My own reflection in the glass is a little less impressive. If I didn't know my own reflection, I'd assume I was one of the hobo's who slept in Hell's Kitchen Park.

The cab lurched forwards, pushing me back into the seat a little further than I'd hoped to go.

"Pretty nice digs, bro. When d'ya move in?" Ash smoothed his blonde hair back with a well-manicured hand that made mine look like they'd been smashed by bricks too many times. Which they had. He had artist hands and he knew it. The vain prick admired his cuticles in a bemused fashion, like he was wondering what colour to paint his nails.

"Three years ago - stop that!" I knocked his down harder than necessary.

"I'd know that if you took my calls once in a while," He crossed his arms and leant back into the seat like he was in the back of a limo. "How's Morgan?"

"Fuck you." I counted to ten and when the rage continued to bubble I counted to ten again. And again. And again until we'd been quiet for a long time.

If there was one thing Ash wasn't it was a fighter. He knew well enough to leave me once he'd pushed my buttons and Jesus did he like to push them.

All twenty minutes later, after we watched the Empire State Building slice past us, I felt calm enough to resume conversation.

"Morgan's fine. Much better now she's clean and tested negative for any kind of STD." I counted again.

Five minutes later and we arrived at the medical examiner's office where they'd taken the body of our baby brother.

The street was empty, bar the cars parked overnight and the usual work trucks that seemed to constantly buzz around the city, doing God knows what.

A gust of wind actually shook the cab, carrying on down the street and through the bare tree branches that were all to reminiscent of death. Bile rose in my throat for the second time this morning. Suddenly that enjoyable taste of cigarettes from earlier tasted like the trees and the air.

"Before we go in there are you going to be able to keep it together?" Ash buttoned his coat up to his neck and paid the driver a bill that looked to exceed the tab. The driver didn't offer change and Ash didn't ask for it.

"As long as the others step the fuck off I'll be OK. Let's just get this over with."

*

It wasn't the family reunion we wanted but it was what we got.

Out of all of my brothers Billy was the last one I thought would get killed in some grotesque manner but life always liked to sour the lemons.

He'd been a good kid. Cheeky, sure, but it was a charming way and he had been so skinny and short it was easy to forgive him for just about anything. When he finally had a growth spurt and shot up to 6"4 the year he turned 17 it was harder to see him as just a scrappy kid anymore but no one hated Billy, then.

Sadly, like all of us unlikely street urchins, he also grew into his talent of ticking off the wrong people and not getting out of the way when the bullets started raining.

"Well look who washed up looking like Father Monroe!" Liev stood up from the dank metal folding chair that lined the hallway and strode over to greet us.

"Fuck you." I could already tell this would be the most used phrase of the whole ordeal.

The woman at the desk looked up under heavily drawn eyebrows like it was the worst thing she'd ever heard. I wondered if she knew she was sitting feet away from dead criminals. Life ain't peachy.

"Right, you hate us all, yada yada." Liev backed off and nodded to Ash as he sauntered past to greet the others.

We were seven brothers. Six now, I guess.

Raised by the aforementioned Father Monroe in the Bethlehem Home for Children. A fancy name for a run-down orphanage. It had been a sweet deal for a while. The seven of us had not a soul to rely on in the world but we found each other. Quite the motley crew.

Monroe took us on like some special little project and promised to keep us together no matter what; even at the cost of our right to families.

At the time we thought it was a great feat. We could always be together because no one wanted to adopt one of us when we were contracted as a group. Then came the change of system when fostering became an option. Suddenly there were rules Monroe couldn't get around so he took us away to a place he found in, hidden in the bowel of Hell's Kitchen.

I've looked into the orphanage since and heard there was a fire in '72 that ripped the place to the ground and they never rebuilt. I guessed that's why they never came after the old guy who basically kidnapped seven young boys.

It's not like he was a bad guy but things took a turn when we did what we did to get by and those things weren't often inside the lines of the law. We'd been raised to fear God but we also feared hunger and death so we stole and then we prayed for forgiveness.

Monroe eventually turned to the drink and disappeared one night under the cover of not wanting to hide from the police anymore; as far as I was aware none of us had heard from him since.

Not that I kept in touch with anyone either.

"So who has the least obscured version of the truth?" I looked around at them, wanting to see a reaction to the verse we'd heard so often from Monroe after we'd been caught with our hands in the missionary box.

As expected Benji was the first to crack.

"We don't know what happened, I swear, man." He could never keep his mouth shut and he was never great at keeping secrets which is why Monroe looked to him first and why I was now. Fucked if I knew how I could take after someone not blood related.

"Will someone just tell me why I'm out of bed at this ungodly hour to identify the body of my brother?" Clenching my teeth never stopped me from the rage that was always bubbling beneath the surface so I did what my anger management coach told me to do; find something which makes me relax.

I got out a stick of gum from my pocket and folded it into my mouth, finally ridding myself of the stale smoke. Chewing, for some reason, always made me calmer. Must be why those old hicks out in the country chew tobacco. That and the addiction.

"The hell you thinking, coming in here with that attitude?" Luke, the oldest of the lot of us with the back hair to prove it, stepped up.

The others immediately took a back step and the desk woman shot daggers before her eyes flicked to what I assumed was an emergency alarm.

"*I* was just feeling like *I* got a call to say my baby brother is potentially dead and now maybe *I* am having a hard time wondering why *I* am stood out here with you all when all *I* want is to go home." Employing statements with 'I' was another anger management trick my coach had me do.

There was no doubt I'd bent the policy a little but it sure as hell made me feel better.

Ash's giant hand slapped Luke's chest to push him away from me. I hadn't even realised how close we'd gotten, and how close the desk bitch was to hitting that alarm, but I could pretty much count the anger lines that ran across his head. That part of me that liked to think of the pain I could cause wondered if those lines ran all the way through his head like the age rings in a tree.

Of all of us me and Luke had the most tumultuous relationship. That was a word I'd learnt from an early age; how Monroe would explain it.

Even after Ash's dick dive into my relationship with Morgan I still counted him higher in ranks than Luke just because Ash at least had the decency to be semi-apologetic after he'd screwed me over, literally.

A door next to the desk opened and an old guy in a white lab coat which announced him as 'Dr. Lami', with him came the scent of sterilisation which always set my heart pounding.

"You are all here to I.D John Doe?" He spoke with an upper state accent which put him at odds with us immediately.

He seemed to notice that when he looked up to see six full grown men in various states of social leveling before him.

I hated that I was the one who looked like the bum from the park when I was the only one of us all who'd finally got their shit together; finally living on the level.

"What do you mean, John Doe?" I turned to Ash at the exact moment a cop walked through the door. A cop I knew all too well.

"None of us have seen him yet." Ash said quietly. His annoyance at the new arrival didn't go unmissed by me. For once we might be on the same page.

The new information took a few seconds to trickle through to my brain but it couldn't comprehend it.

"But we know it's him, don't we? He had I.D on him-"

"No I.D, no teeth, no fingerprints, nothin'" The cop answered, keeping his head down and not looking at anyone of us directly.

He pushed right through our group, striding down the hallway in that purpose driven way he always walked. We followed as a group like a backwards version of the fellowship from Lord of the Rings. All the reasons in the world to stick together and yet we'd all rather be anywhere else.

"Who invited Officer Dick?" Liev practically snarled. It was only when Ash composed himself the way he did before anything; smoothing his hair, straightening his cuffs, that Liev attempted to do the same although he couldn't keep that shit-sniffing scowl off his face.

Under the flickering lights everything was grimmer, my stomach churned. A weaker version of myself would have puked at what was to come.

We followed the doc and our uninvited uniformed guest down a short hallway, the air getting stale and fresh at the same time which sparked more alarm bells and my stomach clenched in protest. The last time I'd felt this was the day my relationship with my brothers ended once and for all.

"I was the one who got called in on the case, and I'm actually a detective now, not that my promotion will mean shit to any of you." The cop stopped and opened the door that led into a place so brightly lit it seemed in bad taste.

If I thought the temperature outside was ball-freezing, then the temperature at the threshold to that room was cold enough to shrink your prostate.

"You'll always be a beat cop to me." Liev wasn't great at being cool-headed so his snotty comment just sounded pissy, like a kid giving adult lip.

We all trailed into the room, like a well-rehearsed lineup.

"Deadbeat, more like." Benji clapped Liev on the shoulder.

I lingered. Sucked in breath. Ran thought all my anger management tools in my head one by one. My gut was telling me to leave now before whatever we found in that room changed me.

"Don't take it too hard, Jack, you know what they're like."

Jack's hand idly rested on the gun on his hip and I pretended like I didn't notice and that I was standing around to be nice or something. I wasn't.

Put it off. Put it off. Put it off.

My old mantra returned to me like a steady drum. I could row to this for a while.

"It's hard to forget. I'm glad you got out Saul. Man, if it had been you out there I don't know that I'dve had the decency to call the others." He ran his hand through his cropped hair, the light catching the grey that had started to colour his temples.

Shit, when did we get so old?

"And I'd appreciate that... look, before I go in there, I need the details. What are we looking at here?"

Jack had been one of us, once. A kid with nowhere to come or go. We'd spent time in the orphanage together but when the place burnt to the ground and Father Monroe whisked us off into the unknown Jack had been one of the unfortunate few who'd been rehomed out of state.

To any other kid another move might not have seemed that much different. There were always kids coming and going from the home for whatever reason the adults deemed reasonable; mostly it was kids they couldn't scare into submission with their promises of divine justice.

For us, though, kids from New York, moving out of State was like moving to another planet. We were born and bred.

Like a lot of kids like us, Jack had bounced from one family to the next until a cop and his wife took him in and adopted him despite his colourful rap sheet of misdemeanors which had usually involved seven other kids. From there he'd followed in his adoptive father's footsteps and a line had been drawn between us.

He moved back to the city and we'd crossed paths, all of us. It was never pleasant.

Young, looking to impress his superiors and clean up the streets he'd romanticized in his absence. And us; a group of criminals who'd garnered a pretty bad reputation. It was a recipe for disaster.

"I can't tell you much; ongoing investigation and everything, but I can tell you what you'll see; burnt fingertips, teeth pulled, beaten to a pulp and no I.D on him when we dragged him out. This was a professional hit, man, I haven't seen anything like it in a long time... brutal, I mean."

From the look on my face, he could tell he'd said too much.

"Shit, sorry..."

"No, you're right. I'm gonna see it anyway. Shit. What did Billy get himself into this time? He was a low-level thief he didn't get into anything deeper than maybe a few computers off the back of a truck."

It didn't make sense. The morning was starting off on the wrong foot in absolutely the worst way. Bad feelings that got worse were not my usual breakfast.

"You've been gone, Saul, you've missed something. Look, this is on the D.L, but Billy got himself on some pretty serious contact lists in the past few years. Someone even linked him to the Garuda gang recently..."

Yet another reminder of why I severed contact with them all. The Garuda gang were in pretty deep with the cocaine trade, there was even talk of them being involved in black market deals and people trafficking.

"Billy and the Garuda? You gotta be shitting me, Jesus! What, and the others all know?"

Jack didn't get a chance to answer other than shrug in one of those 'maybe I know more but maybe I can't tell you' ways.

"You coming in here or you bailin' again?" Luke grabbed me by the collar and hauled me into the room. I decided ripping his arms off and beating him to death with them wasn't the best way to retaliate so I counted to ten. Again.

Jack closed the door, the metal hinges groaned like they knew what was coming. Even the walls could tell the drama was about to start and they closed in around us, trying to get a closer look.

Every hair on my body stood on end. My coat lacked the warmth it should have offered but I pulled it closer around me anyway. I saw the others do the same. Even Ash, in his fancy suit and calm exterior, shuddered.

Chapter 2

There was no real procedure. The doctor seemed hesitant to pull the drawer out of the wall and then, when he had, he stalled again. His eyes betrayed his unease at the situation. No doubt it wasn't normal for this many people to come and identify a John Doe, he probably thought he was in the presence of the mob.

When Jack nodded and the white gauze was pulled back the six intakes of breath were proof of why he seemed like he wanted to be anywhere but here.

It was probably normal for brutally beaten bodies to pass through a city morgue. New York, in particular, wasn't exactly known for its passive population, but this... This was something else.

In all my years living the life I used to live I'd seen my fair share of damage. Dealt it, mostly. That version of myself, my life, was all in the rear-view.

Still, nothing prepared me or my stomach for Billy's body, or what was left of it.

Savaged. No, that wasn't strong enough a word. Looking at what was left of my brother it was hard to pick anything other than 'sick'.

"Jesus fuck." Matt spoke for the first time. I'd avoided looking at him, mostly because I felt the most guilt at what had gone down between us.

His pale complexion paled even more as he took in the sight of the body. All of our faces mirrored the grief we felt. In that moment we were brothers again.

It wasn't long before it was shattered.

"You see what happens when we don't stick together? You did this." Luke came at me faster than I could have expected.

His fist connected with my jaw and I went down hard.

"You son of a bitch!" His foot connected with my face before I could even defend myself, blood filled my mouth which was just fucking fantastic.

"Hey, hey take it outside you two..." The doctor had backed into a corner way behind Jack who I could see was reaching for his gun. Even with my head spinning and a mouth full of blood I could tell he was itching to pull it.

"Don't bother," Luke shook his hand which made me feel better. He'd never been the heavy man, hopefully my jaw broke his fingers, "Take a good look at what you've done."

He spat at me and left which was better than our last parting so by the time I'd counted to ten a few times I felt a lot better.

*

The blood stopped soon after Luke had left, probably because bleeding in front of my dead brother felt in poor taste.

"He took this hard, Saul, just give him time." Ash tried his hardest to say the right things and to keep the peace but I knew him too well to take it as gospel.

"He's a dick and time isn't going to change that. It just might make him a bigger dick." Matt pulled the cover over Billy's body but I could still see it in my mind. I doubted I'd ever forget. "That's him."

The ringing in my ears was jarring and I saw Jack exchange some words with the doctor before the guy scurried from the room like one of those giant street rats that could kill you, given the chance.

"We're taking off." Benji kept his eyes away from the slab where Billy lay.

"Gonna see if we can catch up with Luke, see what he wants to do." Liev didn't even stop to apologise for taking sides. He left the room with Benji hot on his heels before I could even call him a coward.

"What he wants to do? Christ, the best thing any of us can do is keep as far away from this as possible." The threat of my old life creeping into my new was enough to make the pain in my jaw explode again, like a fresh kick to the face.

"Some of us aren't so lucky, bro." Matt hung his head and followed the others out of the room.

"And you, Ash? You gonna get your hands dirty on this one?" I didn't care. I don't care.

"What was it Father Monroe always said?" Ash asked as he took his leave. "Auribus teneo lupum?"

Always one for the dramatics he left without waiting for an answer.

"Holding a wolf by the ears"

It had been Monroe's favourite saying. I'd never much understood the relevance but he had often said it to himself like he was reminding himself of something. Whatever Ash had meant was as lost on me as whatever Monroe meant. I'd never been one for higher thinking.

"Hold on..." Jack was pushing the drawer back into the wall but I grabbed his shoulder. He tensed and I wondered if, for a second, he considered just shooting me there and then.

I pulled the covers back and looked at Billy again. His face was mottled, swollen and wrong. His good looks had been transformed into those of a monster from a movie.

I picked up his hands, the dead weight was all wrong, it was odd that the absence of life would make him heavier. His fingers were black and burnt in a way I'd never seen.

"I know you won't listen but... don't do it, man." Jack used to look out for me. He'd watch my back whenever we were up to no good. This didn't feel like that kind of helpful warning. "I'm just saying, don't do it."

*

I decided to walk as far as I could before my feet gave out before I hailed a cab. It was about fifty blocks back to the apartment. I'd be happy to make it to twenty in the cold.

Getting caught up in Billy's mistakes wasn't on my agenda. I'd worked hard to get away from all of that. Jack was on the case, I fully intended to let him solve the whole thing, there was nothing I could do. I couldn't regrow Billy's teeth, un-burn his fingers. I couldn't bring him back to life.

I made it to Grand Central before my legs tired and my brain buzzed with everything. It was almost six and the sun glinted off the buildings like they were on fire in another life.

The streets were starting to get pretty busy which was the last thing I needed. Even as I looked for an escape route, I saw a young guy in an NYU hoodie walk past with his hood pulled over his head. He had a huge coffee cup in his hand and the way he hustled down the street like he had nowhere to go but somewhere to be made me think of Billy.

If the last hour hadn't just happened, I would have sworn it was him, I would have turned and walked in another direction. Now, I couldn't take my eyes off this young kid who would probably never end up dead and dumped into the ocean before his 30th birthday.

The tears started before I could man up and stop them. It wasn't like I was against crying but these were the kind of tears that made you shudder from shoulder to shin.

I ducked into a side road and into a doorway for a burnt-out department store. Breathing seemed like the hardest thing to do and Luke's words echoed in my head, over and over.

Maybe if I'd stuck around I could have stopped this from happening. Sure, Billy had made his own decisions but what would have happened if I'd have been there for him?

Before I could flagellate myself further a girl with short bleached hair and a few inches worth of black roots stopped in front of me. She was typical New York grunge right down to the trashy doc martin boots. Apart from that and the studs that littered her ears and face she was pretty cute.

"Got a light?" She dangled a roll up between her black chipped nail polished fingers. She wasn't even wearing gloves. Or a warm enough jacket, for that matter. The holes in her skin tight jeans worried me because I'm apparently suffering from young-onset old age.

"I just quit."

There was something I didn't like about this girl. I mentally checked my pockets, trying to remember where I'd put my wallet and phone so I could give myself a pat down later.

"Right, so that's not a post nicotine glow you've got." She smiled sweetly but it came across as sour as spoilt milk.

"That's probably a post-morgue glow." I muttered. It wasn't in my nature to make people feel awkward but the nerve of this girl sparked a part of me I buried away with the aid of nicotine patches, bank account monitoring and anger management lessons.

"You a cop?" She took a step back like it was infectious. There was something in the way the light hit her skin that made me rethink my initial dislike. She was old enough for me to admire her attitude but young enough for me to possibly regret it the next morning.

"Why would you think I'm a cop?" I looked down at my clothes; I was still wearing sweat pants under my coat and my boots were on the way out. Not even an undercover officer would go out looking like this.

"You just have an edge, besides, why else would you be at a morgue this early on a Monday morning?" She produced a small metal tin and tucked her roll up inside.

I didn't know if she was being obtuse on purpose so I gave her a few seconds to figure it out. It was cute how her cheeks flushed when she clocked my red-rimmed eyes. Whether it was real sincerity or because she had decided I was a good mark after all, she took a step back towards me, closing the gap quicker than I anticipated.

"Holy shit, I'm a fucking bitch." She placed a hand on my shoulder, it was the light touch you'd give a stranger and it held a promise I might have collected on once upon a time. "No one close, I hope?"

I couldn't make this any better for her. It was comical, in a way. Here I was, grieving, and yet I was trying not to hurt her feelings. This was a big day for my inner rage.

"It was my brother; we weren't close, don't worry."

She pulled her hand back like I no longer warranted emotional support, biting her lip in a way that showed she knew how things like this normally went.

"Hey, listen, let's go and get a drink. Do you need a drink? I think you need a drink." She talked fast and bounced on the balls of her feet. The way she was looking around made me nervous, like she was expecting someone to come around the corner and bust us. It dawned on me she could be a hooker. I hoped she'd made better life choices than that.

"I'm both on the wagon and also thinking it may be a little early to be hitting hard liquor."

Her energy had changed from nervous and apologetic to something else. The survivalist in me could hear Monroe reminding me to leave any situation I felt unsafe in; I'm sure I could take her if she turned violent but if she had a pimp I might be in for a world of pain.

"it's cliché o'clock somewhere... come on, I'm buying, there's this great bar just down there..." She turned and pointed towards an alley way.

The funny thing is when you're a New Yorker you knew that it was a legitimate option that a bar might be down an alley. You also knew that people tended to get murdered in them.

The girl craned her head around again to look back towards the busying street towards Grand Central. I saw, along with her piercings, a strange tattoo on the side of her neck just behind her right ear. From my quick glance it looked like a tiny monster or gargoyle like you'd see on the side of a church. They'd always creeped me out.

"No, really, I gotta go - thanks though." The time to leave had presented itself and I wrapped my coat tightly around myself and made a move towards the business crowd. "Hope you find a light."

"Maybe I'll see you around." She called after me.

I very much doubted it seeing as I tended not to spend any time this far uptown but I waved anyway.

It wasn't until I was in a cab that I looked back just to see if she was still there, maybe waiting for another guy to scam but before the driver joined the bustling traffic, I saw she was talking to a pretty giant looking dude in dark clothing. I couldn't make out his face but he looked like the sort of guy who could literally punch my face through to the other side of my head. That was a close call. Another reason to remember why I cut my brother's out of my life.

After a highly erratic journey I arrived back at my apartment in one piece but when I reached for cash to pay the driver my hand hit empty pocket. The call wasn't as close as I'd thought.

My wallet had obviously taken the girl up on her offer for drinks.

Lucky for me I knew the secret code cab drivers used in instances like this.

"I'm gonna need to call my girlfriend to pay..." I grabbed my phone from my pocket, just thankful the peroxide thief had taken pity on the crying man in the street and only stolen his wallet.

Before I could dial the driver turned around and squinted at me through the finger marked glass between us.

"You're Billy's brother, right?" He was relatively young for a cabbie, probably mid to late 20's with a jaw most guys would rather not admit to being jealous of.

"Um... yeah..." I took in his face, trying to place him but I'd never been good at remembering people. Places, numbers, debts; they were my strong suits.

"Gio," He pointed to his driver I.D like it would clarify things. "I knew Billy from a few years back. We ran DVD's... totally legit, you know, no stealing or anything. Kind of lost touch. Can't believe the news."

"You heard already?" News traveled fast, especially this kind of news. I had no doubt the rats were jumping ship.

"It's big news; that ain't no way to go, no way man, and Billy of all people. You gonna find who did this?" He was almost fully turned around now, his brow furrowed in what I assumed was real concern. On the street you were a hustler but you were also part of a family.

I sighed.

"And end up like he did? I'm outta that life." I scrolled through my phone until I found Morgan's number.

Looking up at the building I could see our blinds were open so she was awake and no doubt waiting for me with her patented look of anger.

She was going to demand information. I contemplated lying but she always knew. Hell, if I knew how. I'd played enough poker to know I didn't have a tell but Morgan had supernatural powers of truth.

"Hey man, count this one on me. Condolences and all that." He was a sharp one, at least. Rio clicked the doors open and saluted me. "Hope they catch the bastards."

*

I waved to him as he drove away, happy to know that Billy had at least one decent friend over the years. Sometimes my faith in humanity was restored in the most obscure places.

When I got to the front door I grabbed the handle and shook it with all the built up aggression from the morning. The only reason I stopped was because I heard the sound of something cracking.

If I gave a hard enough yank I probably could have ripped the door right open; the fact my keys were in my wallet meant that was an actual option but giving my rage that kind of external release was bad news.

"Locked out, huh?" Mrs. Grimsdale from the apartment beneath mine stepped up behind me with two bags of groceries under her arms. Fresh flowers and bread poked out of the top like hidden treasures.

"Trade - entrance for muscle?" I took the bags from her and gave her my most charming smile hoping she hadn't seen the outburst.

It always boded well to keep her on side, I found. Especially when other residents of the building complained about the noise that came from my apartment on occasion. She was old enough and ballsy enough to carry a lot of weight with the landlord.

"Good day at the market, Mrs. G?" Small talk wasn't my best trait and yet here I was, my second attempt of the day.

"I suppose... It's almost tourist season so the crowds are growing..." She opened the door and I followed her to the elevator. She hit the button for the 3rd floor.

I tried to take my time, helping her unpack her groceries and put everything away, but even going as slowly as I could without looking like a psycho, the time came to go home.

The elevator ride was too quick, despite recent complaints by other tenants to the landlord stating otherwise, and when the door dinged open I wished I could just collapse into y bed but Morgan was waiting right at the door, saving me the need to lie about why I would have needed to knock.

Something about the interaction with that girl seemed troublesome, and it wasn't even because she'd stolen from me, in fact, that part was expected. If I told Morgan she would worry but if I lied she'd rip into me like a category 5 tornado.

"Hey..." She wrapped her arms around me before I could think. It felt so good to be home, back in the world where my brothers didn't ruin every aspect of my life anymore. "Got your text, I can't even believe it. How was it?"

"You don't even want to know." I grabbed her and lifted her off the ground, she smelt of almonds and cinnamon rolls. She wasn't even mad that I broke the news to her that way which was both cowardly of me and also stupidly nice of her.

Despite her look of annoyance she was trying to hide she patted my arm and I let her feet touch the ground again but only because she'd asked. If she let me I'd wrap myself up in her all day, every day. If there was one thing my old life was good for it was bringing her to me.

"Tell me."

Taking my hand, she led me into the kitchen and I laid it all out for her. Every detail seemed gross in hindsight, like a cheap bar that seemed kind of acceptable at the time but when the lights came on in the morning you wondered how you hadn't noticed the piss stained floors before.

"Oh Billy..." She was too good for my family. "He was always the good one, how did he end up..." She buried her face in her hands, potentially to hide how her face would betray her words.

She really didn't like Billy all that much but I appreciated the lie.

He'd been there when she got hit, once. Ancient history. He hadn't lifted a hand to help, even when she was wiping the blood from her nose.

He really had been a good guy but he just didn't *do* anything with that good nature. It was like he couldn't be bothered to live up to his potential.

"That's just their life, you know that. We both know that. Thank fuck we're out." I grabbed her hands and lifted her face up. Her dark hair fell away and I drank in her dark skin, the way it seemed to have been poured over her like melted chocolate.

Chapter 3

The rest of the day dragged on. Morgan left for work at The Color Box, a local hair salon. She'd worked her ass off training and building this life I'd be damned if I let our old life, or rather *my* old life, pull her back down.

A hot shower and nicotine patch later I contemplated my predicament. Getting new keys and credit cards wouldn't be a problem but the whole ordeal felt unresolved.

I'd been mugged before and I'd done my fair share of mugging when I was a kid. I don't know, maybe the game had changed since I last played but for a hot girl to engage in conversation and take my wallet when it was me who'd walked away... something didn't add up.

The phone ringing in my pocket reminded me that my life couldn't stay on hold which was a blessing in disguise.

Billy was gone, I couldn't change that, but I had to do what Monroe always told us to do when we were younger. Compartmentalize the emotions, remember what was important and for the love of all things Holy; keep moving forwards.

Somehow the day had gotten away from me. Work started at 3 and here I was dripping naked with a patch on each arm, staring into the mirror at my sad-sack reflection.

Sometimes I did that. Possibly too often. It wasn't that I wanted to look at myself, more like I had to check to see if I was still me. It was a hard thing to explain, Christ knows I'd tried when I first started going to therapy.

I headed over to The Pony Bar to start my shift; Happy hour started at 4:20 and I was the lucky SOB who'd been put on the rota.

When I walked in I could tell Mrs G hadn't been lying. Tourists were dotted around with the tell-tale maps, scrolling through the camera roll on their phones, picking the best filter for their online bravado and sitting in my bar with a look of mild nervousness mixed with naïve hope that New York was going to be the place they always dreamt of.

I pulled my cap out of my back pocket and slung it on backwards. It was an ongoing joke with me and the others that if my cap was on backwards I was ready for battle, aka don't poke the fucking bear.

I watched as a few of them raised their eyebrows at each other as I walked past.

"Bad day?" Jerry, the manager, was serving a yuppie from out of town one of our pretentious crafts. The guy's eyes watched at the glass filled like liquid gold. I wish I could feel that sense of excitement at the sight of beer. Being on the wagon sucked.

"You bet." I laughed to ease the tension. Jerry laughed whole heartedly and slapped me on the back. Betting; another wagon I was on. These past few years I'd managed to repress every single thing that caused me to fall into my main life trap; anger. Hence the management.

The day turned to early evening and the usuals came and left along with the unusuals that New York had to offer when the weather turned frosty, driving the rats indoors for warmth.

"Bet you could use that drink now?" A small tap on my shoulder from someone reaching across the bar.

I'd turned to restock glasses Freya had brought from the dishwasher. She'd been on duty all week as punishment for getting trashed last week whilst on shift, jumping on the bar and yelling 'Coyote Ugly'.

She had balls, I'd give her that. She'd shown up every day to make amends. Poor little thing from the suburbs looked like butter wouldn't melt but get a drink in her and she turned into a totally different person. I got that.

It took all my strength not to drop the glasses – I was a hair trigger and everyone who knew me knew not to sneak up on me. I looked around to see the blonde punk still leaning across the bar, her whole body stretched across to reach me so her legs were in the air behind her.

"What the fuck are you doing here?" I pushed her back over the bar and signaled to Jerry that all was OK when he glanced over, his whole face creasing into the frown he saved for kicking drunk kids out.

She had the audacity to smile and sit down like she hadn't stolen my personal belongings just hours earlier. I'd never hit a woman before but right now the exception seemed to be staring me in the face.

Count to ten.

"I wanted to return this, I think you dropped it." She handed me my busted wallet which was barely holding itself together. She was deadpan which made me even more doubtful of her intentions.

I'd met girls like her before; young, self-assured, too old for their time and yet so young it hurt to look at them. She was street-wise, or at least she thought she was. What she lacked in experience she more than made up for in bravado.

I'd known someone just like her years ago.

"Right, you're telling me this just fell out of my coat pocket? The pockets that are so deep I can't even find the lighter I dropped in it last week?" I slid the wallet across the bar and tucked it in my back pocket, as far away from her hands as possible.

"Yeah." She sat up straight and leaned her elbows on the bar like she was an old patron. She had a metal Zippo clasped in her hand but I could see an engraved cross design between her fingers. It was mine. "Anyway, I thought you said you quit?"

I watched her hands unclip the lid of the lighter, ignite the flame and put it out. She did it a few times over and I watched for a moment like I was hypnotised, both trying to calm down and trying not to get enticed into the dangerous game she was trying to draw me into. I knew a honey trap when I saw one but god-damn if this wasn't the sweetest I'd seen in a long time.

This time I counted all the way to twenty.

"Hey! No smoking." Jerry yelled across the bar, he looked at me like she was my responsibility, which she was. Bar rule: Your customer; your problem. "You wanna smoke you go outside and stop bothering my staff."

"Relax, man, I'm getting a drink!" She called back to him, not even worried that he was three times her size in muscle alone.

"Well I'm going to have to see some -" Before I could finish she'd thrust a driver's license in front of my face.

"Do you think I've never seen a fake I.D before... Chastity? You have to be kidding me." Her picture was recent, as proof by her hair being bright white with no signs of the black roots that she had now. She looked young, though, the way the camera had bleached her already pale skin she could have been a ghost. The only life was in her eyes which shone with an otherworldly spark in an otherwise muted picture.

"We don't pick our names, Saul..." She snatched the card back, the colour on her cheeks returned like it had this morning when she'd heard it was Billy's body I was identifying. At least I knew she wasn't totally unflappable. "Besides, do you really want to turn me away when I have a proposition for you?"

I felt bad for her if she had to come all this way just to score a new client. The other bar patrons were looking at us now. Her whole appearance was intended to draw attention.

She was a flame in a dark night; her piercings were small but many which already gave her the appeal of 'other' but from what I could see she had changed into very tight pants that laced up at the front with a black bodice that was tight in all the right places and drew your eyes to all the wrong places.

I made a point of never letting my eyes stray below her lips, which were painted dark red.

"Forget the drink so I can keep my job. I'm going for a break; meet me out back." I waved to Nick who was on bar with me to let him know I was taking five.

Chastity was out of the front door before I could tell her to wait so we didn't look suspicious, that way maybe Jerry wouldn't have grabbed me by the arm on the way out.

"Think about it before you do anything stupid." He pinched my arm a little too hard.

"Relax, she's just a kid. I'm gonna direct her to the shelter." I lied, I don't know why, I just did. Old habits die furiously hard.

Jerry shook his head but said no more. I'm sure I heard him mutter Morgan's name, like I needed reminding I was the luckiest damn bastard in this city to have her.

The alley behind the bar was dark and stank of rotting garbage but it wasn't all that bad. The cold air was a blessing in disguise. In the summer it was impossible to take a break out here for fear of being eaten by the rats that gathered for the *really* rotten stuff.

Chastity appeared from the shadows like it was an art form. She'd at least put a jacket on; leather, like she'd be seen dead in anything else. Her breath fogged in the air and mingled with my own which sent a shiver down my spine I couldn't attest to the temperature.

"This isn't what you think it is." I pulled out a cigarette from my pack and bit it between my teeth before I remembered I didn't have my lighter.

Chastity lit her own cigarette and then waved the lighter at me, teasingly.

When I went to grab it she lifted it over her head which drew me into her. I prised it from her grip and lit my own before putting it with my wallet. It had sentimental value but I wasn't about to tell her about It.

"Funny, I was about to say the same thing." She nodded to my lit bad habit, "thought you quit. Liar, liar..."

"I don't inhale."

"Where's the fun?"

If anyone came back here we'd look like we were flirting. Maybe we were. The day was getting stranger and more depressing as the seconds ticked by in derivatives of ten.

Telling her there was no fun in it would only darken my mood and her light attitude. For a reason I couldn't pinpoint I was drawn to her. Maybe it was that she was light in a world of darkness, one I'd been stumbling around in for so long even though I had Morgan. Even though self-hatred was as familiar to me as my own reflection, it still stung when I remembered I wasn't really any better than my scum bag brothers, just better at trying to do better, but I failed at that on a daily basis.

Billy's death only reminded me that I could never really get out of it, only away. What chance did I have of keeping a normal life with Morgan when my brothers were literally just around the corner, doing their same old dance until it got them dead.

"The fun is seeing how long I can go before taking a drag." That was actually true, though I hadn't meant to say it out loud.

"Well aren't you a glutton for punishment?" She finished her cigarette and threw it to the ground like she was angry with it.

"I have to get back inside in a minute so do you want to tell me why you traipsed all this way, without the bull shit about returning my wallet?" I shoved my hands into my pockets to make sure she couldn't take it again.

"I felt bad, ok? You'd just seen your dead brother on a slab and then I took your wallet." She gave me the street kid trick; big eyes, small but warm smile. I didn't buy it.

"Right, so... thanks." I turned back towards the bar. It was too cold to pretend to smoke so I flicked the butt to the ground.

"OK, wait!" She grabbed my arm and my reaction was instant and driven by instinct.

Spinning on my heal I grabbed her hand and drew her back until her elbow was pinched to her side. We were face to face in a second and her eyes were wide. I could practically taste her fear, it was familiar and bittersweet.

"You wait. I don't know who you are, why you took my wallet or why you followed me to where I work but let's get one thing clear; I am not a mark. You do not want to mess with me or piss me off. If you think I'm some chump you can steal from you're mistaken. Go home and tell your guy that if you or anyone else ever shows up on my doorstep ever again you'll both be the ones lying on a fucking slab by morning."

It didn't take much to tip me over the edge. My reserve was gone. I would have to cop to this in my next meeting but for now I forgave myself. It had been a day of hell and I wasn't going to hold myself accountable for burning someone I didn't know.

At least that's how I felt until I saw the tears brim in her overly black lined eyes.

"I wasn't being straight with you, I'll give you that, but I'm not trying to con you so how about you lay off with the death threats you fucking ass hole?" She yanked her wrist out of my grip and took a step back.

Christ, she was young. If I didn't feel like an unstable maniac before, I did right now.

"Then tell me why you're here, quickly..."

Never apologise, that's what Luke had always said. It was a shitty line of action to take but it was one that kept me out of trouble with some. And got me into trouble with others; namely Morgan.

"I was sent to check on you. Someone told me to find you and talk to you..." She took a step back, expecting me to strike again no doubt, but I was too spun.

"Take a hike, kid." I nodded towards the street and backed away from her.

If she tried to come after me I didn't know what I'd do so I made sure to slam the door behind me and I lock it quickly.

The rest of the shift passed slowly, I marked the time only by how many times Jerry shot me looks of disgust; it was over thirty.

Chapter Four

Walking home was a nightmare in itself. Every noise I heard made me jump out of my skin and look over my shoulder. It wasn't a feeling I enjoyed.

There were positives for getting out of that life of grifting and trying to make a buck any way possible but the downside was that I'd gone soft.

Shit, I'd become the kind of guy I would have laughed at. The one who'd walk a little faster if he saw a guy wearing a baseball cap walking behind him. The kind of guy who crossed the street when a group of black guys were walking towards him. It was an embarrassment.

It was almost two a.m when I got to my door and my relief was palpable. I was so tired the thought of my king-sized bed filled me with an irrational excitement and that was before I remembered to think of Morgan and her long lean legs tangled in the sheets.

Before I could click the key in the lock my phone buzzed in my pocket. I jumped out of my skin again and was sure I heard a low chuckle behind me. Looking around I decided it must have been my own subconscious laughing at how much of a pussy I was being because the street was empty.

"What the fuck do you want now?" I prepared myself to hear of another death, another brother succumbing to the street life, as unrealistic as that might be.

"Meet me tomorrow, at the pier." Ash spoke quickly, he was out of breath like he was running.

"What are you doing?" I asked, rolling my eyes when I heard the unmistakable sound of a girl's laugh, "never mind. Why?"

"I need your help with something." He made a sound no brother wants to hear his other brother make. I felt nauseous.

"Whatever it is get someone else. Today wasn't me being re-initiated. I'm still out." I unclicked the lock and snapped it shut behind me, feeling my heart pounding too hard in my chest.

"Come on, you owe me." Ash laughed like I was playing with him. It took all my steely reserve not to just hang up on him. Billy was his brother, too. At least that's what I had to try to remember. It seemed like Ash wasted no time in getting back into the swing of life.

"I don't owe you shit-" I was about to launch into a tirade of verbal abuse but he cut me off.

"I wasn't talking to you, but Saul this is important. Like, life or death. Just you and me like the old days, no one else." He shushed the girl he was screwing and waited for me to say yes.

I didn't want to. I tried not to. Ash was a big reason why I didn't see the others anymore. He'd literally fucked Morgan over until she was so broken and desperate she had to go to rehab. He hadn't been there to pick up the pieces but I had. Letting him back into my life was a mistake but there were forces at work that I couldn't mess around with. Maybe he'd be able to help me find out who this Chastity chick was and why she'd followed me like a stray cat.

"What number?" I whispered as I approached my front door. If Morgan heard this she'd explode.

"Ninety-Two. Eleven O'clock."

The call ended. The number was familiar but I didn't know why. I hated the pier, the smell of water and the crowds but maybe if I entertained Ash for a while he'd leave me alone for good.

I crawled into bed with Morgan and tucked myself up behind her. She was warm on a cold night and when I pressed against her she responded.

*

I woke up at nine in the morning with this gut-wrenching feeling like I was about to commit a mortal sin.

"How are you even awake right now?" Morgan was in a white t-shirt which made her skin look more mesmerising that ever. Even though she had these huge fluffy socks on I found her irresistible. "I remember when my papa died I was in bed for a whole week. I missed senior picture day and had to have one of those anonymous pictures, like the silhouette with a question mark. They could have used an old picture but, no, Marcia Gonzales made a yearbook committee decision to leave me out-" She bit her lip and an apologetic smile pulled her lips up at the corners when she saw how my face had glazed over.

Hearing her talk about her childhood always made me both nostalgic and depressed. She'd been a good girl up until the year she flunked out of college because some guy she was dating got her hooked on coke and pills.

One of my favourite pictures of her sat on the mantle and I conjured it up in my mind; the prim, perfect, typical high school cheerleader with a dimple in her left cheek that used to look cute but now looked sexy as hell.

Despite everything I always pictured her like that, even after she started to look like she needed rehab, years before she actually went. It was astonishing how well she'd recovered. I watched her make breakfast, strutting around like a model right outta the pages of some magazine.

"Stop looking at me like that." She tried to frown but the smile and the dimple appeared as she buttered her toast before pouring us both a huge cup of black coffee.

"Like what?" I grabbed her and pulled her to me, wrapping my arms around her waist to inhale her soft cherry blossom scent.

Her laugh was high and light with no trace of the horrors of her past. That was something I loved about her and something I despised about myself. Every time I laughed I felt like it was a lie, not her. She laughed like it was the easiest thing in the world.

"Like you want to play hookie all day." She peeled my hands from her waist and dropped a kiss on my head. "You want to talk about yesterday?"

Her hand lightly tilted my head up so I had to look her in the eye. It was a trick she'd use for as long as I could remember and it was a bitch. I could never lie to her when I was looking into her dark almond eyes.

"Not right now."

She pursed her lips in thought at my evasion. I needed to see this through with Ash before I could talk about it. If I told her I was still in contact she'd tell me to stop. I'd have to do what she asked and because I'm a dumb ass guy I'd feel like I'd lost. I know I would. If I finished it once and for all I could at least say it was on my terms.

"Right... and why are you up so early today?" It was like she could read my mind sometimes.

"It's not that early." I busied myself with coffee and toast and tried not to think about the pier in case she actually did have the magical powers.

She arched a beautiful eyebrow and mumbled to herself as she dumped her plate in the kitchen sink. The clatter was awful, saying everything she wasn't going to say aloud.

"I just couldn't sleep anymore, I had to get up... I wanted to see your beautiful face in the daytime for once!" I made a swipe for her again when she sauntered past but she wiggled her hips out of my reach.

"Stop working at the bar and maybe we could spend more daytime time together for a change." She smirked and left to get ready for work.

She never failed to mention how much she'd like for me to keep normal social hours but that was just too far removed from my old life. Working in an office, making more money, putting on a suit; these were all attributes Morgan associated with the real world and living clean sober lives.

It wasn't that she was wrong but her reasons for clean living were different than mine and I couldn't bring myself to go the whole nine yards. Not yet, anyway.

With her out of the room I checked my phone. Nothing from anyone. I scrolled through my contact list and stopped at Billy's name.

Billy being found floating like a busted up pinata didn't sit right in my mind. Sure I was sad, he was my brother, for lack of a better term. We grew up together, we looked out for each other. Maybe Luke was right. Maybe I was partly to blame. I clenched my teeth as I resisted the urge to smash my coffee cup.

After Morgan left I bundled up to face the frigid winter air. I had to resist the urge to take some form of protection with me. Seeing Ash and the others again had set of a chain reaction in me that was as difficult to stop as a freight train going full throttle.

The pier was way too far to walk so I took a cab. Unfortunately, fate had decided I'd been received enough hand-outs though, because the cabbie wasn't one of Billy's old friends. By the time I paid the fare I was $50 down and left with sticky hands from the door handle.

Saul found me whilst I was viciously wiping my hand on my pants in hopes that whatever was on my hand wasn't toxic in any way.

"I think the deal is you wipe your prints off what you stole..." He approached with his usual calm and unnerving resolve.

To look at him you might not know he was pretty deep in drugs trade. Or maybe you would, depending on how much you knew about it. The way he saw it was that he wasn't doing anything too bad, he wasn't a mule or a dealer he was just a product manager who made sure things were where they were supposed to be.

"Don't I know it, Morgan's still trying to wash your touch off." There wasn't a moment I didn't hate him for what he did to her.

"Right off the bat, I'm proud of you bro, normally you'd start with the hitting and then move to the talking. That shrink you go and see is really making progress." He walked past me and started to make his way through the small park land towards the water. The smell of musky cologne lingered in his wake.

"Wait," I ran to catch up, counting to ten in the process, "How the fuck did you know I was seeing... he's not a shrink." The feeling of never getting out of the family dynamics washed over me again, like it had yesterday. It was like being strangled.

"I have my ways, look," He spun on his heel and I stopped short. He was taller than me, intimidatingly so sometimes. "I didn't ask you here so I could sign you back into the fraternity so let's get that rant out of the way right now."

His hands were deep in his pockets, gloved no doubt. He always wore gloves like it was his trademark, the bastard.

"You're saying Luke didn't put you up to this?" I had my doubts that this wasn't some sort of secret bid to bring me back on side. Luke had always been the ring leader, we all fell into line behind him. Mostly.

"Luke doesn't know I'm here and, to be honest, I don't think he's all that keen to have you back, man. You left us out to dry and for what? For Mor-"

My fist connected to his jaw before he could utter the second syllable. He went down hard and for a split second I wished I'd made it to ten but then all my rage about Billy's death surfaced along with every repressed feeling I had regarding my miscreant family members.

"Fuck, man, fuck. Stop - stop!" Benji came out of nowhere and hooked his arms under mine until he held me in a painful arm lock behind me. I fought, twisting and putting all of my body weight into my struggle but he remained strong. "You'll kill him."

My fight left me as the anger subsided and I looked down to see Ash on the floor with a bloody nose and his hands wrapped around his ribs. My foot ached meaning I'd kicked him. I didn't remember it; I'd blacked out which hadn't happened in a long time.

The usual shame that came with the anger bubbled under the surface.

"Thought you'd quit." Ash said between spitting blood.

A couple who were walking through the park looked at us with disgust and fear whilst they hurried past. I only hoped they didn't call the cops.

"I have." My hands had automatically reached for a cigarette which I'd lit and slipped between my lips without thinking. The urge to inhale burned my lungs but I resisted. It felt good to withhold the release. "Why is he here?"

Benji reached down to help Ash up. He was shorter and bulkier and I had no doubt he was taking something; his muscles were that unnatural Popeye type that jutted in and out with a disregard for natural body development. No wonder he'd been able to hold me back; in my heyday I'd have torn through both of them without so much as a tin of spinach to help.

"I'm here to help, just like you are." Benji was nervous around me. I didn't blame him; we'd never been that close. Of all of us me and Benji was the most different. Benji and Billy, though. They'd been inseparable. It was only now, looking at him, I could see how the grief had affected him. He looked like he hadn't slept since we got the news.

"Help with?" I could see where this was going. I was already plotting my escape.

"Yeah, well I hadn't got that far yet Ben - see, Saul, we're kind of on a mission..." Ash rubbed his ribs. He sounded winded which made me a little happier about the situation.

"A mission..." He sounded like Monroe. I turned around, sure I was going to leave.

"To find out what happened to Billy." Benji finished for Ash.

I inhaled. The smoke curled through my mouth and licked its way down into my lungs. My head swam a little and then I felt sick and it was fucking great.

"You're out of your minds." I threw the butt to the ground and walked away. The smell of the water in the air was sickening; I wondered how many dead bodies had stewed in that water, lapping against the concrete like soggy, bloated croutons.

Before I'd made it to the end of the path Ash had grabbed me by the arm. When I turned he ducked and stumbled back quickly. I'd forgotten how powerful I could feel, especially when faced with someone who actually feared me. The buzz was better than the cigarette.

"Hate me, hate Luke, but don't hate the others. Especially Ben. You know as well as I do that the others didn't do anything-" He looked over his shoulder where Benji stood starring towards the pier. "He spoke to Billy just before it happened you know."

I didn't know. I didn't know anything about anyone anymore. Ash was right, it wasn't the other's faults. It was his and Luke's and the others got tarred by the same brush because I knew I couldn't cut ties with them and keep seeing the others without the lines being blurred. It was all or nothing and I'd chosen nothing. No, I'd chosen Morgan and I would never regret that.

"He said he was going to find out what happened on his own, you know. He's gotten pretty brave." Ash sounded half proud but I heard the lilt in his voice.

"Billy was brave, too, remember? So brave he didn't care about the fall out and look what happened." I couldn't get caught up in this.

"Normally I'd agree but not this time. Benji thinks foul play." He looked more concerned that I'd given him credit for. It was easy to believe he didn't feel the empty painful chasm I felt at the loss of Billy but maybe I was wrong.

"Of course It's foul play, what, did you think he fell into the water after a night on the town? He'd had his teeth ripped from his skull!" The mental image was burned into my retina's like scar tissue that would never heal.

"You know what I mean." He gave me a meaningful look, like I'd fall at his feet the same way everyone else did.

Benji approached, slipping his phone into his pocket.

"We're good to go." He gave me the same look as Ash but it was a pale imitation. It pissed me off just as much, though.

"Go where?" I didn't really want to know the answer. I was on the edge of the knife; I could fall either way. Backwards to Morgan and a life of hassle free, bartending bliss, or forwards head first into the old unknown.

"Down to the pier." Ash replied.

He clapped his hand on Benji's back and led him towards the waterfront. I knew what he was doing, it was an old trick to temp the other brother into doing what they wanted by leaving them out. Reverse psychology 101.

It worked every time. I tipped forwards, feeling the wind in my face and seeing the life I'd managed to build fly past me like the string of a balloon whipped from your grip by one good gust.

I ran the few steps to catch up and then stuck to trailing behind as Ash led us towards the police tape that created a barrier between us and whatever trouble we were about to get in to. We all looked around as if by some reflex and then we all crouched under the tape. Muscle memory.

Chapter Five

It was hard looking at Benji without seeing Billy; they'd always been partners in crime, Ben and Bill, the terrible twosome. Turns out things hadn't been quite so peachy recently.

"He'd gotten himself into something big, man. Bigger than anything he'd done before." Benji lit a dubious looking roll up and took a deep drag. He offered it out but both Ash and I declined.

"He's right. A few months ago I tried to corner him because, y'know, I hadn't seen him in a while. When I suggested we meet at his place he got... evasive..." Ash led us over to where they'd dragged Billy's body out of the water. There were still traces of blood on the concrete along with little plastic triangles with numbers on. Evidence. That's what my brother had been reduced to.

"Since when is that odd, though?" I didn't want to think Billy had gotten in over his head because then Luke would be right.

"He's never been that sketchy, not with me. He used to tell me about every job he took." Benji looked how I was starting to feel. Lost.

"So, what changed?" Ash bent down and inspected the blood like he was a professional forensic investigator.

When he stood up he looked in the direction of a small squat building that looked like an old boat house that had been hit by a giant storm about 50 years ago and then left to rot.

"He got in too deep?" It wasn't that I didn't want to help but I could see what they were doing and it didn't seem like the smartest idea to me. "Something I think we should consider before we take another step towards that crap shack."

Ash and Benji looked at each other, I knew the look, the one that said they had predicted my reaction.

"But what if we can find out who did this?" Benji was actually taken aback that I might not want to get involved in this. Ash didn't.

"If there's one thing we owe to Billy it's this, man. Don't turn your back on justice."

I laughed out loud. It was cold, I could hear it like I was listening to someone else; even I felt shitty for how much of a dick I sounded.

"You mean vengeance? How many times do we have to kick the shit out of someone for pounding on one of us? How many times are we going to take the heat because someone made a fucking bad decision? I can't do that anymore. I won't fucking do that anymore," I had to clench my fists and count again because I felt a rage blackout coming on. "If this is what happened to Billy what do you think is going to happen to us. This is a message and it's telling us to back the fuck off."

I pointed to the blood, like they didn't see how much of it there was still staining the ground like the remnants of a butchers chopping board.

"We can take anyone on!" Benji fought back. His determination might have impressed me if we were starring in a teen drama about a football team and a sack of shit coach but this was real life and people died.

"You're living in a fantasy, Ben. Life catches up with you."

We stood facing one another; the two of them against me. Somehow I was the bad guy in all of this when I was the only one living a half-decent life.

"Not if you keep running from things, though, right? That's your way out of everything." Ash stepped into my space. We squared off like teenage boys in the school playground. For the first time in a long time I was the one to stand down and I was damn proud of myself for ignoring the burning I felt in my veins.

"Just forget this, forget trying to invoke justice on the world and go back to normal life. At least that way we won't have to identify anyone else in a gross city morgue at shit o'clock in the morning."

The sound of a siren broke the tension, I had to practically hold Benji back in case he dived into the murky depths in a bid to escape. Another reason I didn't miss the old life; the sound of a siren no longer caused me to shit my pants.

"Before you take the high and mighty road you might want to follow me." Ash turned and walked towards the building with Benji hot on his heels. The sirens grew louder.

Inside was just as crappy as outside with rotten wood beams crisscrossing above us like a dangerous cat's cradle.

"Ho-ly shit." Benji dropped to his knees and grabbed his head. He was covering his eyes for good reason.

"How did you know about this?" I took the sight in and felt bile rise in my throat.

The room was dark and stank of decay and death. It was earthy and unnatural at the same time. I covered my mouth with my sleeve in a bid to filter the air but it was no use, the smell permeated everything.

"I got an anonymous tip last night that we might find something here but I didn't expect this. This is grotesque. This is hell." Ash's face paled and for once he looked disheveled despite being the most dressed up thing in the room. His shoes probably cost more than anything that had ever been in this place.

"This isn't right, we shouldn't be here." Benji moved to the door and opened it for the air but he took a step back and let it clatter closed; the cops had pulled up and were walking over. "The cops, Ash, we need to leave."

We looked for another way out but there were no other doors. There was a ramp that led down towards the water but other than that the only dry exit was the one that led to the cops. It didn't surprise me that within twenty four hours of being back in touch with my family I'd now been in the presence of them twice.

"We're not doing anything wrong." Ash tried to use his imposing 'I'm the boss' voice but I had a feeling even he didn't think he'd get away with that line.

There was no use in running so we waited whilst soaking in the sights of Billy's last moments.

Blood stained the floor where a single wooden chair was placed. The arms and legs had chains wrapped around them which is how they must have subdued him long enough to burn his prints and pull his teeth. The rest was just crazy beyond comprehension.

The chair sat in the center of a large circle which looked and smelt like it had been painted in blood. It was crusting and black in places which added to the sickness that churned in my stomach along with my anger.

Inside the circle were strange symbols which could have been runes, I wasn't sure what they meant but they were painted with a ritualistic accuracy which was terrifying alone but there were words painted on the wooden planks behind the chair in a language I didn't know.

'caue, caue-aspiciebat Olymp'

"What does that say?" I nodded my head towards it and the other two squinted to read it in the half light.

We didn't have time to stand around and try to translate it, the cops were getting closer. I could hear them talking on their radio's. In past experience that meant we were in for an ass kicking.

Before they had a chance to storm in with guns pointed at our heads I snapped a picture of the words on my camera phone and swiftly slid it back into my pocket.

"Freeze!" The first armed officer came through the door with a clatter, followed by another. They both had their guns pointed towards us and they moved in silence in opposite directions so they were flanking either side of our little group.

I paid them no mind as I raised my arms above my head. I knew the drill, so did the other two who followed my lead.

Benji even went so far as to get on his knees. I shook my head at him at the same time Ash bit out a laugh.

"Have some self respect, you only go down on your knees when asked, pussy."

Even I couldn't hold back a small laugh, warm memories flooded my idiotic brain. Only a moron would find comfort and pleasant nostalgia at a time like this.

"Why am I not even surprised to find you here?" Jack walked in. He'd been holding his gun but when he clocked us he put it away and motioned for the officers to do the same. "I take it back; Saul." He gave me one of those silent hello's that appeared in a head twitch which I reciprocated.

"You guys can head back to the car, this won't take long." Jack moved away from the door and jerked his thumb at the two uniforms.

"You sure, sir?" The first guy who entered asked, his voice was high and wavered which gave him away as a rookie.

"Yeah, don't worry about it."

We stood in silence as the two left, letting the door swing shut behind them.

"Alright, which one of you is gonna tell me what the hell you're doing on my crime scene? Didn't I tell you to drop it?" He looked pointedly at Ash who just shrugged.

"You know me, I'm curious." Ash had relaxed since the two cops had left, he walked towards the chair and kicked the chains with the toe of his expensive shoes. "Were you going to tell us about this or were you going to keep us in the fucking dark?"

By the end of the sentence Ash had lost his patience, his voice got louder in his anger until he was shouting. Benji had the good sense to grab Ash's arm because in a split-second Ash was trying to lunge for Jack.

"This is an open investigation and, therefore, not something I can talk about with you, *Ashton*, now back off before I have to use this." Jack's hand was gripping the top of his holstered gun. I had no doubt he'd use it if he had to, God knows I would if Ash came at me.

We were at an impasse. I understood why Jack hadn't told us but at the same time my anger was on the rise.

"We shouldn't have come here." I walked away from my brothers for the second time and brushed past Jack who looked and smelt like hell.

"Finally, someone with sense. I'd recommend you both take a leaf out of Saul's book and drop this."

*

Jack's parting words lingered in my mind. I could hear him as I pounded down the street. The day was turning into a good one, finally. The sun was out which made the walk down the waterfront bearable.

"Wait up!" Benji yelled as he ran after me.

"No Ash? Did Jack shoot him?" I smiled in spite of myself. Now that would have been sweet. Not killed, but impaired or maimed slightly. Just enough to teach him a lesson.

"He had somewhere else to be," He fell into step beside me. I couldn't remember the last time we'd been alone together. "that was some real shit back there, huh?"

My response wasn't quick or very eloquent but that's life.

"Yep."

Every time I thought about Billy I cringed inside. The anger of injustice, of thinking of what he could have been feeling and thinking when it happened tore me up and that was before Ash had led us into that room. It was death and torture and it was wrong.

I'd never be able to sleep with that image burned into my mind's eye and, even worse, I was going to have to tell Morgan which was headache inducing.

"You'll help us, right?" Benji was still ghost-white. Violence wasn't his thing, it was mine. To him that place was the worst thing he'd probably seen in his life. Sadly, for me, it was just another day on the job. Or it used to be.

I thought I couldn't feel any worse but that realisation made me hate myself. Really hate myself.

We stopped walking when we reached the parking lot that led back to the street before the highway.

"Look, I don't know what you're expecting from me but whatever it is the answer is most probably no." I reached for a cigarette but found the packet empty; my stress levels rose a few degrees. "I'm still out. This doesn't change things, if anything it makes me realise my decision to leave was the best one I could have made."

Benji lit his own cigarette but didn't offer one to me, which I understood but I still felt pissed about it.

"You're right, of course you are; Saul the righteous. Looking out for number one and forget about the rest of us." He spat at the ground at my feet. "You think that you made the right choice because you're not the one who was brutally murdered? C'mon, you have to hear how messed up that is?"

I did but it didn't change things. Monroe had taught us to stick together but he's also taught us the most valuable lesson of all; get out when you can. Monroe left us when he knew he was in trouble. He never told me with who or why but he told me he couldn't stay and I respected just as much as I hated him for it.

"You can hate me all you want, that's your decision. And this is mine." I saw a cab idling by the roadside like they'd just dropped off a fare at the marina. The timing was perfect, which surely proved there was an almighty power and he wanted me to get the fuck out of here.

"He called me, y'know? Right before he got killed." Benji called after me as I opened the cab door. "He said he found something that was going to change our lives, he said he thought it would make you come home and he was happy about It."

For a second I wanted to go back. I wanted to pull Benji into a hug, give him as much cash as I could, and tell him to leave the city and start over. I wanted him to have a life where murder wasn't a possibility. I wanted him to know that there were people out there who didn't have to steal and con their way through life but I didn't think he'd listen.

Instead of that I got into the car and told the driver to take me back into the city.

Try as I might I couldn't stop from thinking about everything. Billy's death was brutal and wrong but he'd gotten into something way over his head; that was his own doing. Jack was right, this was police business and there was nothing we could do that he couldn't.

The rest of the day passed in a blur. I went to the gym and punched the living daylights out of the old bag that hung in the corner. I must have looked like I was possessed by the devil himself because not one of the guys working out came to talk like they normally did.

When I got home Morgan still wasn't there so I made myself a drink and looked at the picture of the chair, symbols and foreign words that filled me with a sense of foreboding despite having no idea what they said. It was probably because they were written in blood. No doubt Billy's.

The buzzer shocked me out of the trance I'd fallen into. When I looked at the clock and saw I'd lost an hour staring at the photo of the last thing Billy had seen.

"Shit." I got up to see who was at the door, the little screen was black and white and grainy, like the building hadn't been updated since the '50s which was probably true.

"Anybody home?" Liev peered into the camera and smiled like he was having yet another mug shot taken.

I contemplated ignoring him, my finger hovered above the button that would unlock the door. Before I could stop myself I hit it, buzzing him up. My ability to keep them out of my life was waning.

"This is the last time." I had always felt like saying things out loud made them the truth, like a promise to the universe or something. I was yet to see any proof that it worked but it was worth a try. "I will keep my cool. I can be calm."

Whilst I waited for him to climb the stairs I checked my phone.

In the hour that I'd zoned out I had three missed calls from an unknown number, a text from Morgan saying she was going to be late and a few dozen texts from Ash telling me I was a dick, among other things.

"Still scared of elevators?" I opened the door to find my brother pink in the face and out of breath.

It was one of Liev's many strange fears. He also had a thing about cats which was a source of great amusement when we were kids.

"It's not irrational, they can literally kill you. It happens every day." He walked past me and stood in the center of the living room, taking it all in.

This was the first time any of my brothers had been to my apartment. I'd moved here because it was close to my job and far enough away from their usual haunts that I wouldn't run into them by mistake. When I'd text Ash my address this morning he must have sent it to everyone.

Moving again was going to be a pain in the ass but I mentally told myself it was imperative.

"Nice place, so you just had to step over six brothers to get it?" He dropped into the leather armchair I'd found at the market the year before before picking up a framed picture of me and Morgan from the Fourth of July party we'd had at the bar. "It just gets better and better."

Rising to the bait was what he wanted so I counted to the usual ten and reminded myself of the most important thing; getting him and the others out of my life. Again.

"Not that I'm *not* super happy that you've found out where I live, invited yourself over in the middle of the night and insulted me and Morgan within the space of two minutes but what do you want?" My inner fighter was itching to plant a punch right in his face but I held back.

Liev was, for lack of a better word, dumb. He was a petty thief but unlike Billy he didn't get involved in schemes and dodgy deals - he got his hands dirty by breaking and entering, shop lifting and screwing his friends over. He had a severe case of sticky fingers that had landed him in jail for six months when he was eighteen and from then on he acted like some hardened criminal rather than what he really was; a screw up kid who'd been bailed out by his foster parent who happened to be a man of the cloth. That kind of thing really swayed a judge's opinion.

"Have you talked to Matt?" He put the picture back onto the coffee table and fixed me with one of his penetrating stares that would be intimidating if I didn't know him so well.

"Why would I have talked to Matt? I'm trying not to talk to any of you." It was a low blow but it was the truth. "When was the last time you slept or ate?"

Damn my stupid conscience. His thin frame and heavy eyes worried me more than I'd like.

He shifted in the chair and looked away, letting me see the hollow in his cheeks and the stubble that grew in patches like he'd not had a proper shave with a razor in a week or two. I noticed his clothes didn't fit him like they should and he wasn't wearing nearly enough layers for a winter in New York either.

"Are you on the streets again?" I dragged my hand across my face, hating how my heart hurt for him.

"Don't worry about me, I have a place to go." The look in his eyes told me he was lying.

"Let me make you some food."

We went to the kitchen and I managed to put together a half decent sandwich despite having no skills in the kitchen whatsoever.

I watched as he ate it with the vigor of a character from *Oliver Twist*. Leaving him to guzzle a can of Coke and eat some of the cookies Morgan thought she had hidden from me in a jar of dried noodles I went to my closet and pulled out an extra sweater and gloves. When I went back to the kitchen he looked like he'd gained several pounds. He had the look of someone in recovery, I used to see it in the mirror every day.

"Tell me you're not using again."

When he had been released from jail he'd fallen in with a crowd he'd met on the inside. At first he was stealing to fund his criminalistic fantasies; his ideals about how life should benefit those who take what they want. Before long, though, he was stealing to buy dope and then he moved onto the harder stuff. I'd only ever seen two other people completely succumb to their inner-most demons and they both lived in this apartment.

"I'm not, I swear. This whole thing with Billy though... Man, it's just got me on the ropes..." He looked anywhere but at me which made me think he was lying about something but I wasn't in the right frame of mind to probe for more and clearly, neither was he.

"What's that you're working on?" He motioned to where I'd been sitting. Avoiding the truth was something we had in common as a family.

"Oh, nothing. I didn't even notice I'd done that." I slid the paper away from him before he could get a better look. There was a small part of me who couldn't trust anyone anymore, only Morgan.

When I'd zoned out I'd managed to sketch the symbols from the boat house; I didn't even remember getting the pen and paper. I was exhausted.

"Why are you looking for Matt?" I needed to move this on. If Morgan was coming home soon the last thing she needed was to see someone from the past she was trying to forget.

"I just heard from Joel who worked with Steven who said that Matt and Luke were asking a lot of questions about what had happened to Billy... I don't like Luke taking Matt under his wing so much, I mean I love him but he's bad news." The sincerity in Liev's eyes made me laugh out loud.

A few seconds later we were laughing together like old times and my brain felt like it was going to melt. I had this sense of déjà vu. If he hadn't been dead I could have sworn that was Billy's cue to come in carrying some pizza and a six pack of beer he'd been 'given' by 'friends'.

"What's wrong with that?" Not that I didn't care but Luke and Matt doing their own recon really wasn't the last thing I'd expected. We'd always fallen into the same routine of divide and conquer.

"I dunno," He looked genuinely worried about something but he was holding back. "I just don't like that Luke told Ash to leave it to the cops and now he's sniffing around. He's got an angle-"

"Luke's always got an angle. Just stay outta his way... Are you sure you got somewhere to go?" Even if he said no I wouldn't be able to offer him shelter. I couldn't. It was a step back in my recovery. I had to be selfish.

"Nah man, I'm fine. You gonna help Ash and Benji, then? You guys always did stick together, even when Father M left, you guys did your thing..."

Liev had always been the most sensitive and took everything personally, it was a button we'd all pushed. Looking back I knew we'd basically bullied him and even now it was like he was still stuck in the old dynamic. I guess we all were.

"You're not exempt from the gang, it's not like it's all that exclusive," I walked him to the door and tried to be brotherly by patting him on the back. He was bony as hell and I hit sharp, jutting, shoulder blades. I winced and reminded myself of why I couldn't go back. "You should take a break, maybe get out of town for a while. Try a different life?"

It was a long shot but if I could do this one thing for Liev maybe it would make up for Billy's death somehow. Karma and everything.

"And no. I'm not going to get involved. Jack says he's on it so I trust him to do his job. There's nothing we can do that he can't."

He looked at me like he wasn't sure I was joking. When I didn't laugh he got this look in his eye like I'd confirmed whatever beliefs he had.

I counted to ten.

Just before he hit the stairs he turned back. I knew the words before they were even out of his mouth.

"Hey, can I borrow some money? Just until I get a job?" He had already drowned himself in my sweater and buried his hands in the gloves but he still couldn't help himself.

With a flick of my wrist I threw him two hundred dollars which I'd already liberated from my little savings pot by the fridge.

"Stay safe, bro." I waved him off as he trundled back down the empty echoing stairwell hardly anyone ever used. I heard him whistling as he descended.

Before I could take two steps from the door there was a sharp double knock. I groaned; I just wanted to sleep but the night had other plans.

Looking through the view hole I let my head hit the wooden door with a thud.

"You have to be fucking kidding me." My heart hammered at the prospects that ran through my mind. A million scenarios played out; none of them ended well.

Another knock and I looked through the hole again. She looked different than before for a reason I couldn't discern from the small fish-eye view I had. It must have been obvious I was watching her because she looked up at me with big starry eyes and a downturned mouth that was painted red.

"I know you're there." She sounded like she had a cold and when she peered directly towards the circle of glass I was why she looked so different. It wasn't red lipstick she was wearing but blood. Her lip was split and from the looks of it she had a pretty nasty black eye to match.

I hesitated for only a second before I unlatched the door and she barged inside with a force that scared me.

Chapter Six

"No, no, no, you can *not* be here!" There was nothing I could do to stop Chastity from blazing straight past me.

She walked right to the living room; brown paper bag in hand which was hiding what looked like a bottle of whiskey. Great.

"I just - I needed... can I just stay here for a while?" She was bleary eyed like she'd been trying to cry her makeup off. It had partially worked and black streaks ran down her face, making her black eye look more bruised than it might have been.

"No! For one I don't even know you and for two my girlfriend will literally kill you right after she kills me. You have to go." I opened the front door with a prayer that she might recognise that this is bat-shit crazy.

"I didn't know you had a girlfriend." She sniffed and took a swig of the brown bag. Her face was puffy and blotchy and her lip was definitely bleeding now.

"Yes, you did." I knew her type intimately. "You had my wallet, you would have seen the picture inside."

Most people looked away when they were caught in a lie but not her. Chastity actually stared me down. For a moment I was scared she was going to flip and murder me, instead a small smile turned the corners of her mouth up which made me want to kick myself because right then I couldn't stop from thinking how pretty she was underneath it all.

"I just need to lay low for a while..." She didn't take the hint. She was going to make this difficult. "This is a really nice place you have - considering your only source of income is a bar and a salon, just how do you afford this place?" She was looking around but I didn't miss the way her body language had shifted to the girl on the street; the one who was a survivalist.

Explaining my financial situation was the last thing I wanted to do with her and I didn't miss the comment about the salon. If I didn't know any better I'd say it was a threat but it was too early to tell. I might have just been too tired and old habits, etcetera.

"Let me get you something for your lip."

I walked to the kitchen and she followed. I could feel her eyes touching everything I owned like she was cataloging my life. This was my home, this was my new life. A familiar anger burned up in my throat at yet another person trespassing in it.

I handed her a bag of frozen blueberries to her and she pressed it to her lip, wincing when the iciness touched the swelling.

"Not that I'm offering but do you need me to sort this out for you?" I wasn't one to resort to violence anymore but if there was one thing I couldn't stand by and watch it was someone beating on a woman. A girl, really.

"It's nothing, just a misunderstanding," She said from behind the berries. She'd perched on the edge of the counter, letting her leather clad legs dangle. They seemed too long for her body, like she was still in the midst of a growth spurt. "Besides, I don't think you could take him."

It seemed to me like she was goading me but the look in her eyes made me second guess myself. She looked genuinely scared of whoever had smacked her around.

"I'm sure he's a really tough guy." There was no point in telling her I used to be the guy people were scared of in this city. That I was the guy people called in when the first person they hired didn't finish the job. That I'd broken more bones than Elvis had broken hearts. "Wanna tell me his name?"

Chastity shook her head and sighed.

"This is nothing, really. Don't worry about me." She smiled and it was beautiful and flawed all at the same time.

Warning bells rang. I was back on the defensive. She was good but inexperienced in the ways of The Con.

"If I'm not supposed to help you why are you here?" I felt my calm reserve waiver in the face of the danger she posed. If not to me then at least to my relationship. I felt Morgan getting closer like the hand of the doomsday clock ticking every closer to midnight.

Chastity faltered, there was something under the surface. She was scheming but I didn't know what her target was yet. Maybe she had noticed I had more money than she originally thought and she was going to try to take it all. What good was a wallet with a couple of bucks in it when there was a bank account with fourteen million up for grabs? Not that she knew that, yet.

Even though I felt like a dick for roughing up a girl who'd already been through the ringer twice over, if that was even true, I grabbed her by the collar and hauled her off the counter. She didn't even have time to catch the blueberries when they fell from her grip. I let them fall to the granite floor, spilling like marbles.

Even before she could fight back I had her by the arm. Her biker booted feet hardly touched the floor as I hauled her to the door.

"Wait, wait, I can help you with those!" She frantically fought to escape my grasp but I was in no mood to play. My grip tightened as she squirmed to free herself. "I know those symbols, I can help!"

Whatever she was pointing at didn't matter to me. My rage had reached fever pitch and counting to ten wasn't an option anymore, the only thing that would work was eradicating the issue. Opening the door I gave her a hard shove, sending her sprawling across the hallway floor.

"If you even think about coming back here I'll show you how much worse I am than whoever did that to your face."

My breathing came hard and heavy; I could tell she believed me. The look in her eyes was a familiar mix of shock and terror.

With another shove I slammed the door and waited whilst my heart slowed to a normal rhythm. When I looked out of the viewer she was gone, leaving behind only a trace of herself in the form of a bloody smear on the door handle to the stairwell.

*

By the time Morgan got home it was three in the morning and I still hadn't slept despite feeling like staying awake was impossible. It was like a form of self-harm that I just couldn't stop no matter how much my logical mind told me to.

When she walked into the kitchen I was still sat at the counter with the symbols I'd doodled in a trance. I quickly folded it and slid it under a home décor magazine she'd spent way too much money on.

"Hey...Oh." I stood up to greet her but her glare and the empty bottle she was dangling between her fingers like yesterday's trash stopped me dead in my tracks.

"Want to explain this because I *know* you wouldn't fall off the wagon now, I mean, I get why you would but I don't know why you'd do it without talking to me, it's not like I don't understand or like I can't help you through it and why does this jacket smell like cigarette smoke?" She talked fast, overcome with frustration.

Her cheeks were pink which, on her warm brown skin, made her look like a kid again, like when we'd first met. Tears brimmed in her beautifully large and bullshit detecting eyes which made my heart ache in a way that caused me physical pain.

"Honey, wait they're-" I grasped her arms just as she collapsed into me sobbing. Her breaths came in sharp intakes.

"I just don't know why you'd do it. I could have. We went to a bar tonight and I didn't drink but I wanted to," She took a large gulp of air and lifted her head to meet my eyes. "Are you drunk now?"

She sniffed and a tear slid down her cheek. I caught it with my thumb like if I caught it before it could fall all the way to the floor I could stop her heart from breaking like glass.

"No, baby, it's not mine, OK? It's not mine." I wrapped her in my arms and squeezed her gently. It had been a long time since I'd seen this fragile version.

"Who's is it then?" She pulled back and put the bottle on the counter. She smelt like all my clothes did after a shift, smoky and stale, but on her it was like perfume.

It always shocked people to hear I was on the wagon and working in a bar. The truth was that I wasn't an addict like Morgan was, I was just someone who had anger issues and alcohol tended to lead to the person I tried to suppress.

Now came the hard part of the night.

The truth was something we, as a family, skirted around with expert precision. I never wanted to ever lie to Morgan but the past 48 hours filled me with the fear that my old life was creeping in. It was the old life that almost killed her so if I had to protect her from that I would do for as long as possible.

"Liev came over and he brought that with him. The cigarette smell is mine, though. I was wearing that jacket when I went to the morgue and I might have lit up. I didn't take a drag, though, it was more for the nerves." The best way to sell a lie was to use mostly truth.

I slid the empty bottle of whiskey into the recycle bag and it landed with a soft thump on top of all the cardboard. It had been a long time since we'd had glass in there.

"Liev came here? Why? What did he want? What did he steal?" She began running her eyes over every surface. I followed her into the living room where she started lifting cushions on the sofa and pushing things around on the coffee table like she's hidden treasure there that might have been found.

"Relax," I grabbed her hands and lifted them to my lips to kiss each one. "He was just looking for someone to talk to, he's taken Billy's death hard. We talked, he left."

"With?" She eyes me shrewdly, pursing her lips in the way that let me know she knew me too well.

"A sweater, gloves and about two hundred in cash."

Morgan let out a sigh of exasperation and rubbed her eyes making them redder than before.

"I'm going to bed. We'll have to talk about this tomorrow." She kissed me, just a quick one where our lips barely brushed. I was in for a long cold night.

The events of the night replayed in my mind in macro detail as I nursed a cup of green tea at the counter. If I could just keep the real reason Liev was here and the total existence of Chastity a secret I'd be fine. Just fine.

*

It was Sunday, my favourite day of the week for the totally selfish reason that neither me or Morgan were working and nothing to do with the religious implications that still lingered in the darkest corner of my childhood memory.

"Do you think the market will be busy?" Morgan had decided to forget about last night, for now. She hadn't mentioned it yet but I knew she was biding her time. She was always one for perfect moments; whether it was the perfect time to say those three little words or the perfect time to tell you she was feeling frisky. It was all in the details for her so I waited patiently.

"It's definitely getting busier out there, you should have seen the tourists we had in the bar Thursday night. They looked like they'd never seen a pissed off bar tender and a girl with naked ladies tattoos up her arms before."

I tugged my coat on and noticed it still smelled like smoke. I patted my pockets and found the lighter Chastity had taken and then returned. I left it where it was but it felt like I was carry a thirty pound weight in my pocket. I guess that's how much guilt weights these days.

When we'd successfully dressed for the frigid winds that had picked up, we started on our weekly routine.

First stop was always this little shitty coffee and bear-claw vendor who sold high brand coffee at a lower cost. The downside being it was usually burnt.

"Hey Saul, how's things? Sorry to hear about your brother, man, he was a good guy." The vendor handed me my change and patted his heart as a sign of respect but it just made the chill I felt on my skin sink deeper into my bones.

"Thanks Henry!" Morgan came to my rescue when I didn't reply to the sympathies. My words had gotten stuck in my brain. I tried to think of the right thing to say in reply but everything morphed into the blank stare I was giving him right now.

We walked away when Morgan grabbed my elbow and basically dragged me across the street and to the park where we normally sat and ate our pastries, drank our coffees and watched the usual people walk around the usual neighborhood.

Today was different; filled with people who didn't belong here. I instantly felt like I was under attack but from who or what I wasn't sure.

"You ok?" Morgan asked as she led me to an empty bench overlooking the grass. She'd taken a bite already and white sugar powder covered her lips and the tip of her nose.

"Yeah, I just didn't expect Bear-Claw-Henry to know Billy. I guess it makes sense, that coffee didn't fall off the back of a truck and make it into the machine all on its own." I pinched the bridge of my nose; a dull thudding pain started to hammer above my eyebrows.

We fell silent whilst we ate and drank; unusual for us and the tension rose and rose until I felt like screaming might be the only option to break it.

"Do you feel guilty? Is that it?" Morgan dusted her face off and licked her fingers like a kid. She was beautiful in every way, I wanted to protect her and love her until there was no more universe left.

"What? About drinking the coffee?"

She gave me a look to let me know she knew I was playing dumb.

"You've not really talked about it, you've not cried or gotten angry..." The last part was what was worrying her, it was so obvious now, I could see the way her eyebrows knitted together. She'd exploded at me last night because *she'd* been struggling with Billy's death and yet here I was; cold, empty. Maybe my troubles extended further than my normal anger management issues.

"I've been using the techniques. Counting to ten like the doctor taught me..." She didn't look convinced but I couldn't put it any other way. Maybe I was devoid of normal human emotions. Wow, that was a kick in the teeth. "I almost knocked Luke out at the morgue if that counts for anything?"

"But you didn't? You have more control than I do..." Morgan sipped her coffee and watched as tourists wandered past with their backpacks tugged on high. They were the sorts of people who were going to experience what I liked to call a 'New York Carrier' in which a New Yorker carried their belongings off when they weren't looking.

"Only because Ash stopped me, if he hadn't I might have actually bashed his skull in with my bare hands." Something I'd actually done before but Morgan didn't need to know that. She didn't know a lot of things about me. It didn't bear thinking about. "Wait, you said 'do'."

She sighed, when I looked at her she was biting the corner of her lip like she did when she had to tell me she'd 'accidentally' bought a new purse instead of getting groceries. I always allowed her the frivolities because, unbeknownst to her, we could afford it.

"I took a sip of someone's champagne last night when they went to the bathroom..." She spoke in barely a whisper. Her head dipped and she started to cry. This was what she'd been gearing up to tell me, she wasn't about to rip into me for letting my thief of a brother into the apartment and she didn't know anything about Chastity, yet.

"Oh honey, it's OK, it's OK." I grabbed her and pulled her to me, our drinks held at awkward angles beside us. "You're so strong. You're OK."

She wept with her face buried in my shoulder. People that passed watched with idle curiosity; some of the women shot daggers with their eyes like I was being the stereotypical asshole of their daytime TV fantasies.

"I don't want to be that person again, Saul."

If ever there was a time I felt like crying it was when Morgan cried but I had to hold it together.

"And you won't be. Haven't you noticed how good you're doing? So what? You tasted alcohol again after five years of being on the wagon, that doesn't make you weak. A weak person wouldn't have been able to stop. Do you want to drink again?" I looked into her eyes, searching for the answer in the most honest place I could find it.

"No, never, never again." She kissed me, gently and apologetically if you could put a feeling other than desire into a kiss.

I believed her, there was nothing she wouldn't tell me. Sometimes I wished I could tell her everything but even I didn't want to know everything about myself and the things I thought and felt. Monroe had called me 'powerful and destructive' if left to my own devices and he was right. Thankfully Morgan being with me meant I wasn't left to self-destruct.

We wandered to the market and did our usual routine of looking and not buying. In the summer we tended to sell our old unwanted furniture to the stalls and then re-stock with whatever trend we'd been taken with at the time but with the winter months upon us we were holding off. When the cold came in we did what normal animals did; stocked up on food and chocolate.

"I can't believe you bought that chocolate with jalapeño and lime, it's just plain wrong." Morgan laughed as she tucked the bag of candy into the bigger bag which had an assortment of breads inside.

"Don't knock it, you never know, it might be strange but it could also be the best thing you've ever tasted." I ran my hand down her back and let my fingers graze her ass. Her laugh was enough to make me forget most of my worries.

"I just-" Morgan started to say something, her smile on the brink of something else, like she wasn't sure what her next emotion was going to be. "Never mind."

She sighed and became thoroughly interested in an antique stall which had a big collection of old watches, like new ones weren't good enough. It seemed the other shoppers agreed though because in a matter of seconds it seemed like every person in a five-mile radius was trying to elbow closer to look.

A guy jostled me and I turned in time to see him snake his hand into someone's backpack and take as much as he could carry without being caught.

His walk was familiar but I couldn't pinpoint him, his face was masked by a cap pulled low. He limp-jogged away before inspecting his loot. I felt her eyes watching me which brought me back to the stall and her confused gaze.

"What?"

We slipped our hands into one another's and snaked through the crowd to a quieter area covered in geometric patterned woven rugs and bold cushions.

"How are you not looking for justice? How can you let Billy's death just...?" She snapped her fingers, staring at me with her eyes all big and sad.

"Don't do that." I said, gently folding my hand over her fingers. The guy running the stall looked at us from over a magazine and turned away to give us privacy.

"Do what?" She used her other hand to hold me in place whilst I tried to wriggle free.

"The psych thing. I'm OK, really. I don't need to talk about it." I didn't often have to count to ten with Morgan but this seemed like a good exception.

"It's just not like you to not want to get revenge, or at least take it out on someone."

She had no real idea how capable I was of such things.

"I don't understand why you're trying to rile me up. I was doing fine, I didn't want to talk, I was dealing..."

"And now?" She stepped back, possibly because of the look on my face.

"Now I'm fucking pissed." I closed my eyes at the sight of more people swarming around like rats in a sewer. The anger rose to boiling point and I counted and counted but it didn't diminish.

"Maybe you should go home. I need to walk this off or something." I tried not to get angry with her but from the look on her face it was too late.

"OK." She wouldn't even look at me as she took the grocery bags in her arms and weaved through the crowd back towards the apartment and away from the utter dick that was me.

Whatever my problems were, they weren't her but I couldn't understand why she'd pressed me about Billy or getting angry. Getting revenge was something I'd never wanted to consider but now she'd questioned my lack of motivation or apparent lack of feeling a fire stirred inside me.

Whether it was to prove her wrong I didn't know.

I walked and walked, the crowds were maddening. Before long I'd lost all sense of direction, there was just one beacon in the dimness of the crowd; a shock of white blonde hair and a glint of facial metal.

In a flash we locked eyes through the crowd and then she was gone. At a faster pace I began pushing past people, meeting resistance as I went. I took a quarterback worthy hit to the shoulder, when I looked to see who had caused me the rippling pain through my arm I only saw the same guy from earlier limping away; his head bobbed in an alternate rhythm to the tide of people he waded through.

Shoving forward I took off in the direction I thought I'd seen Chastity but couldn't spot her.

Just when I thought I'd imagined her face in the throng she reappeared across the street.

"HEY!" I called but she slipped around a corner and vanished like smoke.

Jogging across the road I left the crowd of the market and the memory of fighting with Morgan behind.

It wasn't long before I'd found Chastity leaning in a doorway, pulling her coat around her lithe body like the thin fabric would protect her from the bitter chill in the air. Her breath was fogging around her, creating an ethereal mist around her grungy elfin features.

"Are you following me now?" She asked. She reached into her pocket and produced a roll up which she lit with her own lighter this time. I made a mental note to stay out of the smoke.

"Sure, yeah, let's pretend that's what's going on and you aren't trying to make my life a living hell." I shook my head when she offered me a cigarette, keeping my distance and my hands firmly in my pockets in case someone I knew saw us.

"You mean you aren't already in hell? Didn't you just lose your brother?" She tilted her head to the side, her icy eyes narrowed at me like she was mocking me.

"Don't worry, I have plenty more." I felt like a dick saying that out loud. It was a thought I hadn't even really allowed myself to think but there it was. The truth to a stranger. Didn't people always say it was easier that way?

"Really? How many more?"

Alarm bells rang again and my initial impression of some sort of honey trap returned. My eyes searched around the area for anyone who looked like a pimp but all I saw was that stupid limping guy hobbling across the road towards us.

"Whatever it is you're doing just leave me out of it. OK? If I see you again-"

Before I could finish the sentence she was inches from me. She was small but there was some power that buzzed around her like an electric current.

"What? If you see me again, what?" She asked, like she was egging me on.

My hands scrunched into fists in my pocket. If she'd have been a guy I'd have probably punched her all the way to Queens by now.

Counting to ten wasn't going to get me very far in this situation so I did the only other thing I could do. I walked away.

I was hardly four paces away before she caught up and fell into step besides me.

"Oh come on, I was just teasing. Stay and talk." She grabbed my arm and tried to jerk me to a stop but all she did was let the beast out.

Within seconds I had hauled her into an alley way between two streets. I pinned her to the wall with one hand around her neck and the other gripping her upper arm. I knew which hand to apply pressure to but the temptation to squeeze was a strong one I'd only live to regret.

"Whatever it is you think you're doing you need to stop. You have no idea who I am and no idea about what I'm capable of, got it?" I was inches from her face, leaning in so close I could smell the sweetness of her lipstick.

She struggled to speak. I barely noticed her hands clawing at mine for relief.

"I know..." She gasped before trying again. "We're the same."

My grip loosened and she dropped to the ground coughing.

A moment of fear washed over me, my head felt like all of the blood had left it; draining away with my self-respect. If I ever told Morgan about this she's be equally pissed and elated that I'd finally cracked.

When I felt the blood rush back to my head I leant down to help her up full of intention to apologise except before I could reach her a jolt of pain from the back of my skull sent me sprawling onto my side. I felt the blood that I'd so recently had returned start to slip down my cheek and through the gap in my lips heating the side of my tongue with its metallic tang.

"Fuck." I spat the blood and looked up in time to see a guy dragging Chastity up by her hair before slapping her to the ground again. She fell like a rag doll. All dislike for her dissipated with my sense of self.

Wave upon wave of unbalanced dizziness washed over me, pulling me every which way like one of those rip tides people warned you about but you still got caught up in them anyway. I couldn't even make it to my feet. It didn't matter; by the time I was on my hands and knees a boot sung towards my face and the darkness of pain swallowed me whole.

Chapter Seven

If I thought waking up to a bed without Morgan was depressing, I was way off. Waking up tied to a chair with chains and seeing the same sickening sight from Billy's place of death was sickening enough for me to feel the bile rise in my throat.

I'd been dragged to a dark room but it couldn't have been far because the sun was still shining through the painted windows. It wasn't great logic but it was all I had.

The room had the faintest stench of paint and iron. From the look of the symbols painted on the floor it was clear where the smell was coming from. A mental scan of my body told me it wasn't my blood so that was a relief.

It was strange to find myself so calm, despite the sickening churning that was happening in my stomach. I guess all the years of scaring the crap out of out-of-luck addicts had hardened me to the antics of criminal beatings.

"Hey!" I yelled as loud as my I could muster. I had no doubt I wouldn't be heard by passers-by but it didn't hurt to expel the anxiety of being tied to a fucking chair. "HEY!"

With my body weight behind me I began shaking until the chair rocked back and forward. In my mind I'd be able to rock the chair over, the chair would break and I'd be free and ready to kick the living shit out of the asshole's who'd hit me from behind. Reality had other plans.

Before the chair could even tilt any way that might have led to the start of the plan a firm hand on my shoulder shoved me down.

"Quiet." His voice was hoarse but it was more like he was doing it to mask his identity. When we walked around to face me I got a sudden jolt of fear, on top of my current level. You might say I was approaching petrified. The guy was tall and built. He was carrying a strange bowl but the thing that set my heart pounding was his face or rather, the mask he was wearing. Pure white and featureless. Not original but it was jarring enough to spark something primal inside me.

When he knelt down beside me I saw red liquid, thick and dark, in the bowl. The paint from the floor. He slid a long, curved blade from his pocket and held it to my throat, the sharpness bit into my skin sending shooting pains down my entire body. The slow trickle of blood that oozed out tickled and stung but I couldn't scratch it. My rage bubbled.

I couldn't help myself; I let out a truly blood curdling scream.

After it subsided the guy moved around me in a practiced motion, stopping at every symbol on the floor and humming strange words as he went as though I hadn't made any sound at all.

It was stupid to think my brothers would charge in right at this moment to save me. I doubted even Jack had any idea who these guys were yet, but I still prayed for it. Waiting.

The masked man moved with purpose; he never broke his stream of mumbling, he didn't even look up when I began to shake the chair again, it was like he had totally zoned out.

There was a moment when I thought I might have done it, might have broken the chair, I even prepared myself for an epic take down; not even caring the dude had a giant knife. I shouldn't have gotten my hopes up. Mid-thrash another hand pressed my shoulder down with a force that told me he wasn't messing around.

"Don't do that." He spoke with a thick accent, but I couldn't place it. I'd never been great with accents. It was European, I knew that much, but pinpointing the exact place wasn't an option. It wasn't like knowing if a guy was from Brooklyn or Queens.

Next thing I knew there was another knife pointed to my throat. It turns out that no matter how many times that happens it still causes your insides to feel like they've sank to your knees along with every ounce of bravery you thought you had.

"Why are you doing this?" These guys had to be the same guys who'd killed Billy.

There was no answer to my question and the knife remained pressed to my jugular, reminding me with every pulse of blood that passed underneath how close I was to Billy and his fate. Blacking out felt like a possibility but I couldn't let myself freak. I was Saul Abraham, half of New York knew to fear the fuck out of me.

I stilled my mind with my anger management techniques and waited for any chance of escape. My thinking was that if I could wriggle free I could take these two guys. Before I'd finished the thought fate kicked me in my gut. I heard the door that was behind me open and the sound of footfall echoed all around. Too many to count, though none of them, bar the guy with the mask who was still chanting, moved into my eye line.

The energy in the room swallowed me whole. Any ideas of escaping left with the bravery I'd been trying to muster. I knew what was coming next; the torture.

"At least tell me why." My voice was quiet, lost in the chanting to the others I hoped, but the guy with the knife at my throat heard. He pushed the cool metal further into my flesh, the burning sent shockwaves through me, making my heart pound furiously.

"caue, caue..." His tongue flicked the words at me with venom.

"I flunked the classics, I know you speak English." I watched as the chanting guy painted a familiar design on the wall, his whole body moved with his hand as he drew it across the brickwork like an expert; dipping his hand back into his bowl before slapping more red on that dripped down so the design looked archaic and deadly.

The group behind started chanting and singing the words that the guy was drawing on the wall, the sound built up and up along with my heart rate.

"Caue, Caue-aspiciebat Olympo, Caue, Caue-aspiciebat Olympo"

When he was finished he turned, the knife the other guy held slid around so that the point pricked the base of my skull.

"Cave Bestiam!" He yelled just at the moment every else's voices stopped abruptly. He glared at me through the mask's eye holes. It was like his eyes glowed with an unholy light; it was clear

this was a pretty insane cult, not just a couple of guys who held a grudge. If Billy wasn't their only target the game had changed.

"Slaughter them all." The group chanted at once, in English so that I'd understand the threat.

The guy with the paint dropped to his knees and stretched forward so his fingertips grazed one of the symbols on the floor like a demonic yoga pose. If Morgan had heard me think that she'd have a field day teaching me the finer points of how yoga could never be demonic. I held onto the idea of that chastising moment, letting it guide me from fear like a beacon.

The knife that had been pointing to the base of my skull fell away, the release of pressure was pure bliss followed by tension.

He appeared in front of me, like an unwanted mirage. He was big, round and heavy looking with thick arms like hunks of meat. He actually looked like the butcher from the deli on 10th. His face was shielded by the mask but nothing could mask his smell, which was testosterone mixed with pickled gherkins.

"We pray for protection, from violence." He spoke, muffled and throaty. He knelt before me, his hand clutching something in his belt.

"You're the only people we need protection from." I didn't like where this was going, especially when the horde behind us replied.

"Vult." It was sharp like a bullet and just as painful. The sound ripped through me like a hot poker and I screamed.

"We pray for strength, from corruption." He pulled a hammer from his belt. Not one you'd find on a building site or in

Home Depot but one you'd find in a courtroom. A gavel made from metal.

"Vult." They shot again, my body felt pain ripple through like an electric current. It was uncontrollable and I found I couldn't move my arms from the pain of it.

"We pray for forgiveness, from wrath." He raised the gavel and my eyes went wide. I knew what he planned to do. He'd snuck his other hand to my left wrist, holding it firmly in place. My hands were curled over the edge of the chair arms, I tried to move but I couldn't force my limbs to react.

As he brought the hammer down on my hand, smashing the bones with as much forced as he could muster under the power of prayer, I screamed.

"VULT." The rest of them replied on behalf of God but it was garbled nonsense, just a noise that existed outside of the pain that engulfed me like the flames of hell.

When he grabbed my other wrist my body reacted out of desperation. A need to survive that transcended the pain. It was like the world had stopped; time didn't exist, just this one moment where everything stilled around me.

"God, no. Fucking FUCK! Stop, please." Tears rolled down my face. People say your life flashes before your eyes when you die. It's cliché to say it does, it's probably cliché to say it doesn't but it just doesn't.

The only thing that you know is the idea that you don't want to die and feel pain but you also want it to stop and be over and you want God to take you or whoever the fuck rips your soul from your body and sweeps it away for an overhaul. I had no regrets at the end, no moment of clarity that screamed in my mind and to the universe that if I survived this I'd be a better man and I'd give money to charity and never curse again. Even Morgan seemed like a distant memory that I couldn't hold onto long enough to worry how she'd survive without me.

He raised the hammer, his eyes glinted with satisfaction. The worst part was I knew this was only the start of what was to come.

"Get off him!" An angel in the dark appeared giving a kick to the guy's head that sent him sprawling to the ground with a dull thud. His neck was rotated at an odd angle.

The next few moments were like a rush of relief mixed with pain and the mental breakdown that came with it.

Even in the waves and waves of agony that throbbed up my arm and into my brain I could tell Chastity had made a mistake. In the fog of my mind her tiny frame was being surrounded by tall masked men in robes. They were ominous and threatening.

She kept them at bay with a metal pipe, swinging it left to right like you would if you were a lion tamer with really shitty equipment. They drew in close and backed away when she swung in their direction but it was only a matter of time before she was overcome.

"Run..." I said, the word came out in a whisper and she didn't let on that she'd heard me. She stood her ground like she was waiting for backup, buying time. She didn't attack or retreat. I wriggled my arms to try to help her but the pain from my shattered hand made me stop. I had to bite down the scream that wanted to escape my lips. The only way out of this was to keep a clear mind but I could feel that clearness slipping away into unconsciousness which I fought with every fiber of my being. Leaving her alone to face these guys wasn't an option.

"Drop it or he's dead." A clear voice put a stop to the circus as all heads turned towards me and the smart ass who'd picked up the knife from the floor next to the dead guy. He held the blade to my neck, his other hand gripped my hair and yanked my head to the side, revealing the target for everyone to see. Surely they couldn't just waste me now. I hung onto the hope that the importance of the ceremony meant we had time to get out of this. If they wanted me dead, point blank, they could have put a bullet in my brain at the market.

Chastity took the situation in. She was smart, you could see it in her eyes. She had a brain and it worked quickly. City kids like us had to know how far we'd go to survive, we had to know when to fight and when to cut and run. She showed no signs of the latter. Maybe she wasn't so smart after all.

"Just go, get out, you'll let her go, right?" Reasoning with insane men was hardly ever a great idea but maybe they weren't ready for collateral damage in their quest for whatever it was they were looking for. "She's innocent, won't God punish you for hurting her?"

I knew it was a mistake to bring the big guy into it a split second too late. The guy's grip in my hair was vice like, I was sure I could feel the follicles bleeding.

"Don't you dare speak his name." He spat in my face and pressed the knife into the side of my neck. This time blood didn't just tickle my skin, it poured down. Hot and deadly with a distinct sulphuric smell that ignited all the wrong parts of my brain.

"You just made a fucking mistake." I bit my lip hard to distract myself from the pain of my hand. I pulled at the chains as hard as I could muster, the idea that I could be hurt even more didn't cross my mind. I don't think he really believed I could do it so when my right hand broke free and I grabbed his knife hand he wasn't prepared for the attack.

Lurching forward I pulled his body weight with whatever hair I still had left attached to my head. His body was on my back and I took the opportunity to guide his hand, with the knife, into where I assumed his head was.

The look on Chastity's face told me I'd hit my target and sure enough, a moment later, the body dropped to the side of the chair with the knife protruding from the side of his neck, the blood on the ground all but washed out three of the symbols painted around me.

It was like a spell had been broken. The life pouring out of this guy sent a shock wave through the others. They began to murmur between themselves, their head honcho was lying at my feet pumping blood out like a burst pipe.

Chastity noticed the difference in their attitudes as well. Like a dog after being neutered they didn't know what to do. With all the bite taken out she swung the metal pipe hard across someone's masked face. It cracked down the side and he grabbed it, groaning.

"Get the fuck outta here before I beat every last one of you to death!" She brandished the pipe like she really could do it. For such a small thing she was as menacing as all twelve of them, at least that's how many I thought I'd counted but it looked like Chastity was in more than one place as well so I couldn't judge my vision as much as I'd like.

Sirens wailed in the near vicinity which made their minds up for them. They made their escape quickly, funneling through the door that was behind my field of vision. A well-executed drill.

When the room was empty I collapsed forwards into myself. My broken left hand was still chained to the chair, my right hand and wrist didn't feel much better and I let myself sink into the relief of being saved along with the reminder of every place my body had been injured. The back of my skull, my hair, my neck, my arms and hands; every inch felt bruised and on fire.

Staying as still as possible made it easier for me to escape in my mind but it was a short-lived reprise. Chastity was at my side, pulling my face up to look at her. I could only just make out her tear stained cheeks and her smudged eyes which were swelling with eventual bruises.

"So brave." I smiled at her as best I could. I knew I'd failed to control my facial muscles when she frowned at me.

"You'll be OK, I called the cops." She took a second to check my neck and hands, undoing the rest of the chains that wrapped around my left arm. "The one who's investigating your brother's case..."

It took me a few seconds to sift through her words; she had more information about me, Billy and Jack than could be possible without some sort of spying.

"Who are you?" I tried to grab her hand but she backed away, looking towards the door that must have led to the street. The sirens had stopped meaning the cavalry had arrived.

"There's no time, I'll come and see you." She began backing away, ignoring my pleas for her to stay.

By the time Jack and his unit came crashing through the doors with their guns and flashlights Chastity had vanished. I let myself give into the pain and the trauma of the events.

"We got ya, bud, we got ya." Jack's face swam in front of me. He called in an ambulance; his voice held no emotion but I saw the horror on his face moments before I slipped into the dark.

Chapter Eight

If anyone ever tells you hospitals aren't that bad they're lying through their teeth.

Waking up with wires hanging off you has a distinct way of making you feel too mortal for your own good. At first the beep of the heart rate monitor seems like a soothing lullaby, you drift in and out of dreamless sleep thinking that it's a small musical bird that must have decided to sit and sing to you at your window, until you realise the sound only exists to hurt you and the incessant glibness is actually the equivalent of a vulture swooping in for it's next meal.

Jerking awake isn't something that just happens in the movies but it is the only place that makes it painless. My left hand is encased in plaster cast. If the pain wasn't so searing I'd possibly laugh at how much it looks like a boxer's glove. There isn't a chance I could do any damage with it; I'd officially been declawed.

As much as I couldn't stand to be lying here like an embarrassed kid after he'd has his ass kicked at school, I was happy about one thing; I hadn't been given any drugs for the pain. It might sound dumb but thank God for small miracles. Just the feeling of pain in my hands and neck reminded me I was still here; through luck or fate I'd survived those crazy sons of bitches.

"Are you awake?" Morgan was curled up in the chair next to the bed under a big coat. She looked so small and fragile. I moved to touch her hand and winced. Right hand wasn't doing too good either it seemed.

Those guys were gonna pay.

"I'm awake, you're here, the world is right again." I smiled, there was no reason not to. Even in a hospital room in a bed that someone had probably died in I was happy so long as she was there.

"I thought you were-" Tears brimmed in her eyes.

"Hey, don't worry..." I motioned for her to join me in the bed and she did, curling up against me like a cat.

"What if the last thing we said was in an argument?" She sobbed and buried her face in my shoulder. Her hair smelled fresh and alive, her body was warm, nothing else mattered.

"Then I guess you would have felt really, really guilty so how about you make up for it and you take me home and look after me, maybe we'll get you a nurse's outfit?" I held onto her with as much intent as I could with two injured hands. Joking aside the idea that we almost lost each other again scared me more than anything else.

"Am I interrupting?" Jack knocked on the door and leaned casually against the wall like this was an everyday occurrence. Maybe it was for him.

"Yes."

As much as I wanted to give the guy a hard time, he'd basically saved my life back there so now I owed him pretty big. From the look on his face I could see he knew it, too.

"No, come in, I was going to grab a coffee anyway. You want anything baby?" Morgan unwound herself from me and floated to the door on a cloud of relief. The last coffee I'd drank had been before the attack and even though I was thirsty the thought of drinking anything right now made me sick to my stomach.

"No, you go, this won't take long."

When she'd left Jack pulled the chair up to the side of the bed and made himself comfortable. That was when I saw the uniforms outside the door, flanking it like they were protecting it, and in turn me, with their dipshit lives.

"Those guys friends of yours?" I flicked my head towards the door as pointing was yet another thing I found I couldn't do.

It wasn't that I hated all cops, I'd just not had great experiences. When Monroe liberated the seven of us from the orphanage we'd been forced into hiding for a long time whilst he got the papers together to show we were legitimately his kids rather than the state's property. Adoption papers were hard to come by, even more so when they were fake. From an early age we'd learned not only to avoid the police but to lie to them at every turn just to cover our tails.

"They're gonna be friends of yours real soon, too, Saul. You've been appointed a protection detail whilst we stoke up the investigation. Consider them your guardian angels." Jack leaned back and quickly rectified his positioning like he'd been hit by lightning. "We're gonna get these guys, I swear it."

I didn't know if I could take his word for it. He looked sincere but there was something old worldy about those guys that made me doubt his abilities. They were organised and I had no doubt they would have ripped my tongue out, or something. If Chastity hadn't shown up to wreck their party I would have been on a hard slab rather than a lumpy bed.

"About that, did you find Chastity?" The look on Jack's face meant she'd got out unseen and, hopefully, unscathed. I wasn't sure how I'd turned this page into being worried about her, I guess it had something to do with her saving my life.

"Chastity? Did I find- look, you've been hit pretty hard, at least one to the back of the skull, you're probably gonna be confused for a while." Jack looked towards the door like he was worried I needed to be put in a medically induced coma for being crazy or some shit like that.

"Yeah, sure, let's pretend I've lost my mind whilst I was being held by the totally sane men in white masks who were literally going all cloak and dagger on my ass and praying to God for some shitty forgiveness they sure as hell won't be getting anytime soon," Jack hit a nerve and a familiar buzz thrummed in my chest, "Who called it in? Who told you where to go?"

Trying to keep my cool was getting harder and harder. I could only pray that my normal life with Morgan might be on the horizon, that we could sink back into old routines of keeping our bad habits tied up in the closet. The sad thing was that I knew on some primal level that I was coming out of retirement and I didn't have the balls to admit I liked it.

"Anonymous tip from a payphone a block down from the building. Some young thing called me direct on my cell and said you'd been taken by some, and I quote, 'psycho dumb-fucks' who were going to sacrifice you to...something, what?" Jack stopped and frowned at me like I'd really lost it.

"That would be Chastity," I was smiling, maybe it *was* the concussion. "she saved my life."

"Whoever-she-was didn't stay to make a statement so she's top of the list for leads, you got a last name...an address?" Jack got a pen and pad from his pocket and held it poised and ready.

"No, man, I don't know her..." If this got back to Morgan I was dead in ways worse than today's events.

"Right so some girl, who you don't know, calls me up on my personal cell phone and tells me you, by name, is in trouble and needs help from the guys who killed Billy... your brother?" Jack scribbled her name down anyway. "You do remember I'm a detective, right?"

There was a commotion outside the door, shouting and the usual sounds of rough housing that came with the arrival of my brothers.

Jack got up and clapped me on the shoulder harder than he meant. I bit back the urge to scream and punch him and he quickly moved out of arms-length like he knew my thoughts.

"You want me to let them in?" He lingered between me and the doorway, teetering on the edge of a decision that I was supposed to make.

Apt, really. Tell my brothers to take a hike; pretend everything is normal and go on with my life despite the fact that someone had just tried to kill me after killing my brother or let my brothers into this room and then my life, again, to get revenge or whatever it was they were looking for.

"Don't you need to ask me some questions?" I knew the drill. You were questioned, even when you were the victim, until you felt that you were actually the one on trial. OK, maybe I had a chip on my shoulder about cops still.

"We can do that later, you're not going anywhere and I know you won't be coerced into a false statement by them so we're good." He rested his hand on his belt, his fingers brushed the grip of his police standard gun. "You know I never had a problem with you, man. After the fire and you guys took off it was never about you..."

It looked like he wanted to say more but things were getting too close to actual emotional interaction so I saved him the embarrassment.

"Yeah, man, I know, I know." I'd learnt a while ago that if you wanted to put an end to a conversation or argument you just repeated the other person's sentiment. Sometimes it would save your ass and other times it would have the total opposite reaction and result in a broken nose.

Jack took the high road and nodded his silent thanks. He walked past the cops stationed outside my room and whispered something to them. The next thing I knew there were five angry looking guys stood around my bed, vying for blood.

*

Luke was scarily quiet whilst I relayed all the gory details. He only chipped in when I attempted to gloss over Chastity. There was a reason I was trying to protect her from everyone, there had to be. It wasn't that I was doing it on purpose but like there was a deep cavity in my brain where it was trying to hide her.

"So this girl you've never met before broke into the building, took on a room full of crazy religious nut jobs, called Jack and then took off?" He glared at me, his usual way of seeing if someone was telling the truth. Intimidation went a long way for him.

It wasn't a great story, I knew that and I knew if my brothers could pick a hole Jack would dig a fucking trench but it felt like the right thing to do.

"She looked like a stoner so she was probably using the building as a crack den."

"A junkie who called the cops-" Matt typically backed Luke up, like the little lap dog he was.

"Not just the cops but Jack. Something doesn't add up," Liev countered. He was stood at the barred window, looking down on the miserable winter's day. "She must have been following you."

I breathed a sigh of relief that they didn't automatically think I'd lied to them, stupid brother trust. It was great they still had it but the part of my brain that was the old me and missed the family unit died a little bit.

"You can't stay on the sidelines anymore, Saul, this is too important and too dangerous." Benji had that gleam in his eye which told me he thought he had me over a barrel.

Each one of them glared at me with their own level of intensity but none shit on my parade of useless neutrality than Ash, whose look of indecisiveness mirrored my own in a way I couldn't comprehend.

"I think it's time you came back into the fold." He drew a card from his pocket and flung it at me. "Starting with this."

I looked down and found something I'd been holding onto for a while now but hadn't had the guts to really look at.

"Where'd you find this?" Anger swelled, betrayal burned, all of the other negative emotions I'd spent years trying to bind down with pathetic rituals and mental training were closer to the surface than they had been in a while. This is what my brothers did to me, this is what my old life did to me. The threat of becoming the man I'd begun to loathe was enough to make me sick.

"I found it in one of those gloves you gave me." Liev lied. I knew exactly where I'd hidden it, from myself and from Morgan, and it wasn't tucked in a glove in my closet. It was no good calling him on it, though, here was the truth and the old life crashing in like the tide.

"I haven't called him. I haven't seen him. Christ, it might be a prank for all I know." I threw the card into the air, Luke snatched it from flight and glared at it like the card itself had caused him personal insult.

"So where did it come from?" Luke passed it to Matt who slid it into his jacket pocket like the secretary he was. Fucking whipped.

Truth was I didn't know where it came from. Someone had slid it under my door one night whilst I was sleeping. I'd woken to find it face up with the name and number glaring up at me, as threatening as a knife to the throat.

"I found one at my apartment and then another at the bar, left next to an empty glass I found when I was clearing up... I don't know who left them and I don't want to know." It was easier to fight against the tide when that's what you were used to doing. It was muscle memory.

"He might know what's going on," Benji, ever the optimist, said. "To think, all these years I'd assumed Father Monroe had kicked it"

I was doubtful it was really him. Sure, Monroe had left; a true Irish Exit, without so much as a goodbye, but after recent events I was even less inclined to call the number that was scrawled on the card in bold black italics.

Before Billy was killed, before I'd been attacked, I was hesitant to know where Monroe had been all these years because the truth had never been a friend to me. I'd thought long and hard about it when his name reappeared like a letter bomb. There was nothing he could say that would make his disappearance OK, leaving us like drowning rats in a city of dirt, death and despair. We'd just about held on with him acting as our moral Fagan, trying to keep us on the straight and narrow, but with him gone the family fell to shit and for what? Nothing he could say would make it alright.

"I don't want to know if it's him. I don't need to know it's him, I just want to go back to my life." It was through gritted teeth I said it. The pain of the beating I took was only getting worse as I became more aggravated. My head throbbed as much as my hands did. I knew I'd pass out but right now it wasn't soon enough.

"*We* need to know. We need to understand this... this insanity. This isn't normal - I saw Billy's end, are you telling me what happened to you was unrelated?" Ash was barely holding it together. He was either really protective of me all of a sudden or else he was starting to worry about his own hide. After the past few hours of my life I'd say it was pretty fair if it was the latter.

I hesitated, I'd told them what happened but I'd glossed over two pretty important factors. One of them was Chastity and the other was the symbols. I wasn't sure what to make of it, my brain was trying to block them out but I saw them every time I blinked. It was a tie between me and Billy that lingered like his ghost. It was like he was here, trying to show me something, trying to point me in the right direction but I couldn't understand him.

"The symbols were the same but there was something different... I'm too tired to think about it. Can't I just get some fucking sleep?" There must have been a look in my eye which told them I wasn't kidding because they all kept their mouths shut.

My eyes started to close without my permission, like I was being dragged away from the room.

"Let's go, come on guys." Ash herded everyone out and one by one the room felt calmer, the air cleaner. "We'll be back when you're feeling better, brother. You have to take this seriously, you can't sit on the sidelines... what if they go after Morgan?"

If there was one thing about Ash it was that he was great at seducing you with words and ideas. He could say just the right thing at just the right time and he'd have you caught in a bear trap without even realising it.

By the time I drifted to sleep my dreams were filled with scenes of Morgan's death. Each time the blade sliced her skin it felt like physical punishment. A couple of times her wounds shone like bright white sunlight was hiding under her skin. Sometimes she was an angel, with wings as pure as her soul. When they cut them off her with shears she bled the brightest red I'd ever seen and the blood pooled into ancient symbols like the ones they'd painted around Billy and me.

Chapter 9

"Do you really think it's a good idea?" Morgan asked. She helped me shrug my coat on in preparation for the winter air. It was known to bite at this time of year but I welcomed it right now. I'd been cooped up in the hospital room for three days and fresh air, no matter how frigid, was a blessing.

"No." That was the long and short of it. Morgan yanked my sleeve a little too hard and my arm exploded in pain.

Both of my hands were pretty useless but only the left was broken. Fractured, actually. In many, many places. I cursed but counted myself lucky. At least it was only my hand and not my face.

"Saul!" She opened the door for me and pushed me into the hallway. She wasn't the most gentle of carers.

"You know I don't think it is so why are you asking?" I felt like a terrible human being for taking my temper out on her. The hospital told me in the morning that my bill would be posted to me and I was pissed off I'd been forced into their care in the first place so paying $15,000 for someone to fix a hand was insanity. They might as well have reset my hand into a permanent flip of the bird so that I was reminded of them every time I looked at it.

"I'm sorry, I didn't mean it," I wrapped my arm over her shoulders as we left without a backwards glance. I knew without looking back that the cops were still on my ass, even when we got outside a patrol car idled at the sidewalk behind the cab Morgan had called for us. Ash said he'd send a car for us but I'd told him to back off. "I'm still not sure. I don't want what happened to me to happen to anyone else, especially you."

Morgan nodded but kept quiet as she helped me crouch into the back of the taxi. It was harder than you'd think when you couldn't use your hands.

"What does Jack say?" She asked when we were in motion. I watched her face as she gazed out of the window, watching the buildings go by. The snow had begun to fall and threatened to smother everything it touched like a disease.

"The usual," I laughed, thinking about his warning after he'd taken my statement. "He dropped by this morning to check up on my discharge and reminded me that the investigation was being dealt with by the police and he could really use my help to keep the others out of it."

Jack looked at me this morning like we were on the same side but the truth was I still didn't know if we were. I didn't know if it was still a case of me against them like Jack seemed to think it was. There was more to it now. Way more.

"So, you're going to stay out of it?" Morgan tilted her face towards me but kept her eyes on the streets like she was looking for someone; a shadow that might appear to kill us both.

"No. It's gotten too dangerous, whoever they are, they're out to get us. Maybe all of us, I don't understand why..." I checked the driver wasn't listening. When he honked and gestured to the guy in the rusty old pickup truck who'd cut us up I continued. "It's up to us to find them. If we have to kill them we will, Jack can't be involved, it's not his fight."

Growing up we'd always had the mentality that when it came to our family you fought until you couldn't fight anymore. When Benji had been locked in juvie for a string of arrests regarding whores and the potential pimping of said whores we fought it, knowing he'd done wrong.

In the end it didn't matter that he'd made the mistake, it was up to all of us to fix it and we did through a string of favours and fallouts. This was the same.

"So, you do think it's a good idea?" She lightly slapped my leg and a small smile played on her beautiful lips.

"I didn't say that." I placed my bandaged hand in hers and she ever so gently wrapped her fingers around it. I kept the pain out of my face as best I could despite the fact that any touch was agony.

"What if it gets too dangerous?"

We rounded the block to our apartment and the cab driver pulled up. Looking over my shoulder I saw the police car stop a little further back. If I was following someone I'd sure as hell have spotted them by now, it was a sham. I wondered whether they were doing it on purpose but it was a fucked-up tactic if that was the case.

"Then I'll scrape all the cash I can get together and we'll high-tail it to Bora-Bora or some other crazy fucking place in the world and we'll live out the rest of our lives alone and happy, how about that?" She liked the idea a lot, she smiled and it lit up the back of the dingy vehicle like a summer's day.

Like my brothers, Morgan didn't know about my secret bank account which contained millions of dollars. A parting gift from Monroe. It was one I'd never asked for and one I tried not to use unless times really got bad. It could have been illegal money. Who am I kidding, it was most definitely illegal money.

Even though he was a man of the cloth Monroe wasn't what you'd call trustworthy. The older we got the worse he got for lying, violence, and everything else that came with it. It was obvious the money was as dirty as it came, maybe that's why he was back. If it was him. There were so many unanswered questions my head was like a pinball machine except the pinball was a grenade and someone had pulled the pin.

"Keep the change." Morgan handed a cool $40 to the driver before he drove away.

"Woah! You forget we have a hospital bill to pay for?" We were fine but I couldn't let her know that. Little secrets were OK, that's what I had to tell myself.

"I've got it covered, I got more appointments than a gyno after spring break, we'll be OK on one salary for a while, right?" She held the door open and we walked up to the apartment. I'd never missed my own bed so much in my whole life.

"Hey, even if I have to glue rags to my hands and wipe tables all day I'm going to work tomorrow." I wasn't about to go stir crazy now I'd been freed from the confines of observations.

Morgan frowned at me but didn't say anything else about it. She was no doubt biding her time, waiting to show me how much of a useless lump I was going to be. I didn't give a fuck. Being kept in a house was too much like being in prison. I was a free -ange kind of guy and those holier than thou mother fuckers weren't going to keep me inside.

"Can we just forget everything right now and get into be-" I stopped talking at the same time I stopped walking.

It was as though some primal instinct had kicked in. If I were a dog my hackles would have been raised.

"What is it?" Morgan tensed at my being tense, stepping behind me for protection. I won't lie, the feeling it gave me was empowering. It was a surge of energy that felt like I'd stuck a fork in a power outlet; I was willing to die to protect her.

"Stay back, ok?" I prayed she would do what I asked as I made my way towards our apartment door.

It was when the elevator doors had opened that I sensed a change in the air. It was like I was a Jedi sensing a change in the force and it was fucking strong in the hallway. Like when you could tell there was someone behind you, I could tell there was someone waiting for us in our apartment.

The door was ajar and I kicked it open with my toe, realising probably too late that Morgan would probably have more luck fighting off an intruder. My stupid bandaged hands were no use so I pulled them towards my chest and mentally prepared to body barge whoever was waiting for me on the other side.

The feeling of invasion didn't disappear when I stepped over the threshold, it intensified with each carefully, quietly placed footstep as I crept into my own home.

Remembering my techniques to fight the internal rage was difficult in most situations but this was a real test. If those masked maniacs wanted to jump me on the street, fine. Coming into my home was another thing altogether but I did my breathing and remained as calm as I could. It was a lie to myself. It might have been a way to keep the aggression down but it was also fighting mentality. A calm mind would always win in a fight against one filled with unkempt rage. I had to pretend to think I was doing it for all the right reasons but whilst I controlled my breathing the truth about what I was prepared to do was crystal clear.

A few more steps into the hallway and I would be in the living room. I knew, within a second, that there was someone there.

The best attack is a surprise attack so I pretty much threw myself in, expecting everything except what I was met with.

"Holy fuck! Chastity?"

I ran to the heap on the floor. There were books and mail from the side table on the floor, all smeared with blood. Next to the mess was Chastity, black and blue and beaten so badly I didn't know if she was conscious or comatose or potentially dead.

"Saul! What's wrong?" Morgan ran into the room holding a can of pepper spray like it might jump up and bite her. She was poised and ready to go on the attack but she stopped in her tracks at the sight of me crouching over Chastity, my useless hands hovering awkwardly over her limp body. "What the fuck is this?"

-END OF PART ONE-